King Of The Car Park

Steve Beed

Copyright ©2024 Steve Beed
All rights reserved
ISBN: 9798345248218

Dedication

To Annie, thank you.

To everyone in 1H22.

To all the usual suspects who continue to encourage me – you know who you are.

ACKNOWLEDGEMENTS

This book is a work of fiction, characters and events portrayed are not based on actual events or any persons living or dead.

CHAPTER 1
King of the Car Park

The car park is a constantly changing entity, a Tetris of vehicles in every size, colour, make and model, shifting and rearranging itself throughout the day. Some cars limp in sputtering noxious fumes from dilapidated exhausts, dripping oil onto the tarmac. Others purr in on near-silent electric motors, or growl impatiently as their oversized engines itch to be let back onto the open road.

The owners who disgorge themselves are as varied as their transport: young, old, tall, short, black, white, rushed and harried with kids in tow, sauntering in with all the time in the world to shop. Whole families come along for the outing, merging with couples and solitary shoppers, creating one amorphous group; the customers.

They come from far and wide to stock up on life's necessities, luxuries and myriad other items, even ones that they didn't know they needed. They gravitate towards the aisles, cut-priced goods and special bargain offers stacked on every shelf. Under the bright fluorescent lights, they follow the route that has been carefully designed to take them past the things they don't need to get to the ones they do, as they make their inexorable way to the checkouts.

The wide front doors suck the customers in then spit them back out when they are finished with them, leaving them blinking in the sunshine as they pause to remember where they parked their cars. They hurry home to unpack, store, cook and eat their purchases, before returning to go through the same routine again next week when the cupboards are bare once more.

As each customer leaves, a new one arrives. There is a never-ending flow of bodies traversing the car park, which is perhaps the most transitory part of this temporary destination. The only people that spend any significant amount of time in this cathedral of consumerism are the ones that work here, and even they don't spend a single second longer than they absolutely have to. They have families to go home to, errands to run, appointments to honour and liaisons to keep.

Steve Barclay, the quietly spoken and slightly overweight manager, has to get back to look after his mum, who has dementia. He tries to get back in time to have a short break before the carers leave for the day and his, sometimes long, night begins. Often she knows who he is, but more and more frequently she is calling him by his dad's name, Bob. She has no memory of Bob passing five years ago and is insistent that he should take the cat (also long since departed) to the vets. Steve has no clues as to the origins of this persistent memory and merely plays his part in the daily façade, waiting for the carers to return once more so he can escape to the sanctuary of work.

Sonia from the café has been seeing her boyfriend for nearly a year now; she moved out of her family home into a tiny one-bedroom flat with him last month. She can't wait to get home, change and spend her every non-working hour with him; she is hoping he'll propose soon and is unaware that he has already purchased a ring. He is holding onto it until some nonspecific 'best moment' arrives. He is too scared to offer it as he is convinced she will say no and their relationship will come to an abrupt end.

Several of the younger staff will leave, go home, then meet up again in the pub – anyone's birthday providing an excuse (not that one is needed) to get dressed up and have fun. Most weekends there is an opportunity for socialising, together with friends and partners who do not work at the supermarket. Once they are away from the building the supermarket is rarely if ever discussed, or even mentioned.

Wendy has to get to the police station. She is about to start her shift as a special police constable; she needs to make a good impression if she wants to get on when she joins the force full-time. This means arriving on time, even if that necessitates going straight from work and missing her evening meal.

Nobody is at the supermarket for longer than they need to be. Nobody spends any more time than they have to there - except Tim.

Tim is usually there in plenty of time before his shift begins and rarely rushes away at the end of it. He spends his day wrapped in a layer of bright orange jackets and hard-wearing combat trousers wrangling trolleys, collecting them from all the corners of the parking area – and sometimes further – and corralling them all by the entrance, ready for each new wave of shoppers to use as they arrive.

This apparently straightforward task comes with its own challenges. He has been doing this since he left school and is well aware of the difficulties that will face him each day. There are pitfalls and rookie errors that make this seemingly simple job a more skilled occupation than most people give it credit for. Tim has explained this many times to various understudies and pretenders who had come and gone over the years;

Firstly: respect the trolleys. They are all individuals; they have minds of their own and will try to do their own thing. You have to coax them, not force them or they will invariably turn on you.

Secondly: don't bite off more than you can chew. Know your limits and don't try to move too many at once, or they will rebel. People whose cars get scratched in car parks tend to be quite grumpy, as does the manager when he has to sort out the repairs with the insurance company.

Thirdly: don't point out people's failings. They don't like to be reminded of their foolishness in having inadvertently blocked other people in when 'just popping to the cash point'. Similarly, they are usually aware that they are not disabled or don't have children with them – but it's raining/they are in a hurry/they're only going to be minute - take your pick. Generally people get upset if you mention that their entitled behaviour may inconvenience or cause problems for others.

That was kind of it really, it was a straightforward job as long as you didn't try to embellish it or get clever. Just move the trolleys from here to there, clean them when people mess them up and keep the car park looking neat and tidy. The best part of the job, as far as Tim was concerned, was that there was little or no interaction with other people required, other than watching them as they come and go. It's not that he doesn't like other people, he just prefers not having to talk to them too much. Of course, he would always respond to a cheery hello or a request for assistance with lifting bags into a car. Some of the regular customers knew his name and would ask after his health, and he knew many more people by sight, having grown up in the same town as them.

But most of the customers liked to pretend he was invisible, avoiding eye contact and not acknowledging his presence. It was a game he was happy to join in with as he went about his business. He had been asked many times over the years to fill in for other staff - the indoor workers. He was more than capable of shifting things around the warehouse, stacking stock onto shelves or any of the other jobs inside the building, but they generally involved making contact with people. He preferred the car park where he was his own boss and his own company.

Today was slowly coming to a close. The warm spring air was cooling rapidly and the flow of customers was starting to dwindle, leaving the aisles clear for the evening shoppers who come in before closing, hoping for bargains or trying to fit their shopping trip into the narrow window of time between coming home from work and going to bed. The trolleys left out now would be collected into the covered shelters and locked away, ready for Tim to start herding them towards the entrance again tomorrow.

His last job of the day was to retrieve a broken trolley that he had found earlier. One of the front wheels had buckled after a customer's vigorous attempt to persuade it up onto the pavement, rather than walk the extra few metres along to the dropped kerb. It had been bandoned in disgust at its lack of climbing ability, which meant

Tim now had to manoeuvre it all the way to the delivery area where he stored damaged, broken and worn out trolleys until they were collected and taken away to be fixed or scrapped. The collection wouldn't be until the end of the week and there were already two trolleys from yesterday waiting to be inspected and discover their fate.

Except, when he finally coaxed his latest casualty into the space, there were none. Odd, they never got collected early. He looked to see if they had been moved, he knew they wouldn't have gone back into circulation or he would have found them somewhere, left in disgust at their inability to move in a straight line. His brief search did not reveal their location, shrugging he parked up the newly defunct trolley and went to collect his jacket, bag and flask from the covered area at the side of the building. They were tucked under a small chair that he kept there for when he was on breaks. Of course, he could use the staff break room inside if he wanted, but…. Well, people. He didn't mind the smokers coming out to share his space for their breaks, but had no desire to join them indoors. He made occasional exceptions for this on days when the freezing wind blew cold snow across the open space and it was so bitter even his thermals and several outer layers of clothes and jackets weren't enough to keep him warm, or when he needed the loo.

He nodded goodnight to the security guard, Ahmed, as he passed the entrance, then walked on into the gloom of the evening. The lights on the main road started to flicker into life, illuminating his route home.

CHAPTER 2
How Was Your Day?

It was a nondescript house in a nondescript area. Close to the town centre, in a road full of similar looking semi-detached houses. This was the house that Tim had been born in and lived in his entire life. All of his birthdays, Christmases, sad days, happy days, boring days, days and weeks that blurred into one amorphous mass of days - all piled up on top of each other, first into years, then decades. Inside the front door was his safe place, his sanctuary. Everything was where it should be and the familiarity and constancy of it calmed him in a way that nowhere else could. He had taken ownership of it when his mum had passed away seven years previously, managing to keep on top of the modest bills and upkeep with his wages from the supermarket. There was an insurance payout following his mum's death that had paid off the mortgage and provided a comfortable sum of money that he had yet to decide how to spend, after all, he had everything he needed. Until then it was sitting dormant in a savings account.

He hung his coat by the front door and went directly to the kitchen to put the kettle on and rinse out his flask. He had some leftover stew in the fridge that he put in the microwave to reheat while he went upstairs and changed out of his work clothes. These motions were well rehearsed, familiar from their constant repetition; the routine that followed each working day. As he pulled on his jeans he banged on the bedroom wall, "I'm reheating the stew, there's plenty if you want some."

The answer was silence. He shrugged, put on his slippers and went downstairs to eat at the kitchen table, switching on the small tv on the kitchen counter as he sat mindlessly watching the first thing that came on. It was a programme set in outer space, kind of like Star Trek but without any of the familiar characters he remembered fondly from his younger years; he wasn't hugely invested in it but watched to the end once he had started. He had long since mopped the gravy from his bowl with some bread and butter by the time the closing credits began to scroll up the screen and he got up and started the washing up.

Later, as he was getting ready for bed he thumped the wall again.

"Hey, did I tell you, a weird thing happened at work today? Some idiot's moved a couple of broken trolleys that I put to one side, I couldn't find them anywhere. Why would they put them in a different place without telling me? I'm going to have to go in early tomorrow and try and find them, before they get put back out in the car park and I get customers complaining. I wish people would leave things that are nothing to do with them alone."

He left the thought hanging there as he switched off the main light and climbed into bed, picking up his Ready Player One and finding his place. He read a few pages, but found that he could not focus on the nostalgia of the old arcade games he and Ian had loved so much while his mind was still running through the possible locations for his missing trolleys. Finally he admitted defeat, deciding he would definitely get in early tomorrow and look for them, he settled down for the night, slipping into sleep as the day ebbed away.

CHAPTER 3
Wendy

At the same time as Tim was hunting for his missing trolleys, Wendy was arriving at the police station for her evening shift. The locker room was infused with the perfumed scent of deodorant and a faint underlying odour of well-worn shoes. Whatever, she had been shown the male officers changing area by the jocular sergeant who had given her an orientation tour when she first started. The smell in there had been all Ralgex and sweat, not an experience she had enjoyed. She stopped to look in the mirror before she went out, to make sure everything was in order.

As usual she found it hard to reconcile the uniformed official looking back at herself; it was not an image her younger self would have recognised or imagined. Her brown hair was tied well back, showing her full face without make-up or earrings. She had never really thought she was pretty, but looking back at herself she thought maybe hers was the kind of face you grow into. If it was, she was starting to get used to it at last.

She had come a long way from the dysregulated anorexic 16 year-old who had left school with the bare minimum of qualifications, ready to pursue her dream of becoming a hairdresser. The college course had been more demanding than she had imagined it would be, also the trainers and tutors had expected her to listen and do what she was asked, which was probably quite realistic when she stopped to look back, although it felt unreasonable at the time. The level of cooperation and compliance expected of her had eventually been too much and she had dropped out.

From there she drifted through a series of jobs in offices and shops, never sticking with any one thing long enough to start to rise through the ranks. She had been asked to take on the assistant manager's role in a bakery, but had abandoned ship when she realised it would impinge on her evenings and weekends. The owner of a factory she had worked at had offered her extra shifts and a chance to learn the ropes in the office, she thought he was creepy and just stopped going to work there. It had been like that for years, until she met Rob.

Rob had been the one who had helped her recognise her own ability and intelligence. He was the one who had persuaded her to return to education and fill in some of the gaps in the exam results section of her CV. He had also been the person who had gently encouraged her to start looking for a more permanent job. He had been good for her, which was ironic considering he had now left her, because he hadn't meant 'something as dangerous' as applying to join the police force.

Her decision had been made after a night out with her friend Vicky. An unsavoury incident had led to Vicky getting a black eye and losing her handbag - nothing major, just the run of the mill thing that happens to somebody every day. But when it happens to you it's different, it's terrifying and leaves you feeling vulnerable and tearful. The police officers who had come to hers and Vicky's assistance (mostly Vicky if she was being honest) were magnificent. They didn't just turn up, they rushed to them. They bought an air of calm and reassurance. They stayed with them until the perpetrator had been apprehended two streets away and Vicky's bag had been retrieved, then they had made sure they were safely delivered home.

Watching them work Wendy had known then that it was what she wanted to do. Rob had laughed when she told him about her epiphany, thinking it was just another of her impulses and that she would forget about it by next week. But she didn't, and when she started to research how she could join the force and asked him to look at the requirements with her he realised it wasn't one of her whims and became alarmed. He punctuated his speech with actions, for emphasis.

"Why would you want to do that?" He physically turned his chair around so he was facing her full on.

"It's dangerous." He placed his hands palm down on the table in front of him.

"You'll have to wear a uniform and take orders." He tilted his head to one side.

"You would be dealing with drunks and drug addicts all day." He composed his face into what he supposed was an earnest expression of concern.

"You'll have to do night shifts." He half smiled and chuckled soundlessly.

She reminded him that he was the one who had been encouraging her to look for something better than her current job in the supermarket. She tried to convince him that it was not the same as going to an active war zone and that she would be able to handle it. Finally she asked him, "What's so bad about the joining the police?"

"I just don't want you to do it; you won't be able to; it'll be too hard for you;" he replied, slumping back in his chair and looking petulant and child-like.

"But it's what I want. It's the first time in my life that I've ever really wanted anything. Can't we just see how it goes? I may not even get in."

"No, you have to choose. It's me or the police." Now his expression changed to one that hinted, prematurely as it turned out, that he was confident in his own place in the pecking order of Wendy's life.

There were more words between then and Rob eventually leaving, but those self-centred and derogatory comments were the ones that Wendy remembered.

She nodded approvingly at her reflection, her hair pulled tightly back showed her forehead in all its too big glory and she couldn't help but notice the angle of her nose (a reminder not to try and get into a boat when you've been drinking – but that's a whole different story); self-criticism came easily to her, but overall she thought she wasn't too bad; nothing that she couldn't live with.

It had been hard to get this far, but in 6 months she would be starting her training to become a full-time officer if all went well. She kind of missed Rob, he hadn't been all bad and she wished he had been able to share her pride in her achievement, but wishing things doesn't make them happen. Last she heard he had moved in with a hairdresser; she guessed that was the kind of safe job he would have liked for her. She had considered finding out where he lived now, so she could take the remaining belongings he had still not collected from her flat to him. She knew she probably wouldn't, although the thought of getting one of her colleagues to help her deliver it in a squad car did have a certain appeal.

Her evening shift was a quiet one in the end. She had been teamed up with Mark; grey hair and grey eyes calmly observing, explaining and letting her learn by giving her responsibility in non-urgent matters and gently preparing her for the time that she would be the one who was expected to be a reassuring or threatening presence (depending on who you were and what you had done). Also he hadn't been involved in any of the 'banter' that had greeted her arrival on her first day, and still accompanied each shift.

In fairness, it was mostly harmless, and she knew she was going to have to get used to it when she joined full-time, she was hardening up to it already. But it still hurt a little that she was treated differently from her male counterparts; no comments about their appearance or questions about their love lives, suggestions that she might like to join people for a drink and an unsavoury rumour that there was a sweepstake for who would be the first to bed her – fat chance. Mostly harmless, but persistent and beginning to get irritating. She supposed she would just have to suck it up for now and sort it out once she was chief constable.

After speaking sternly but kindly to a clearly inebriated and cheerfully cooperative young man on a pushbike with no lights, then watching as he locked his bike up and continued his journey on foot, the shift finished. A quiet evening overall, Mark said it was often like that midweek, but not to take it for granted or get complacent.

She arrived back at the quiet, empty flat at one o'clock and slid under the crisp, clean sheets after putting her uniform carefully on hangers and smoothing it flat.

CHAPTER 4
Still Missing

A low beeping sound and flashing light roused Tim earlier than normal, he wanted to give himself time to have a proper look for the missing trolleys. They had been the first thing he had thought of when he had woken up and he knew it would still be bothering him later if he didn't get to the bottom of it. He had a perfunctory breakfast, made his sandwiches and flask up then set off, shouting up the stairs that he was leaving now and would be back at the normal time.

He quite enjoyed his walk to work as a rule. He tended to see the same people most days, walking in the opposite direction from him. Some you could set your watch by, they would pass without acknowledging one another at practically the same spot each day. By the footbridge would be 'Mrs Tattoos' who tended to wear sleeveless tops at every and any opportunity, showing the world her ornate dragon on one arm and a large fish on the other. 'Spider lady' would cross the road as he arrived at the crossing by the corner shop, usually dressed in black with long angular arms and legs that all seemed to be working against each other as she scurried on. 'Mr Fit' usually bombed past him on his bike just before he got to the turning for the supermarket, heavily muscled and pedalling his bike as furiously as if he was in the closing stage of the Tour de France.

Because he had set out earlier than normal he did not see all the usual extras that provided the backdrop to his life. This added to his feeling of discomfort, increasing the wrongness of the day. He knew that he shouldn't let it get to him as much as it did, but it had. In the grand scheme of things Mr Barclay would probably shrug off the loss of two trolleys, or assume that Tim had been mistaken somehow. But Tim was responsible for the trolleys and took a great deal of pride in what he did. No shrugging it off or forgetting it for him.

The trolley job had been his first and only job since completing his education. At first everybody had assumed he had taken it to fill in the summer while he decided what to do next. He had gotten good exam results and could have applied for other, better jobs. His grades were even good enough that he could have gone back and studied some more, maybe gone on to university. But once he had started the never ending job of taming the car park he found it suited him and his purposes, so he carried on.

Mr Barclay's predecessor, Mr Williams, had tried to convince him to try one of the other roles, telling him there were 'always opportunities for bright hard-working young lads'. He had not managed to persuade him; Tim had steadfastly stuck to his role. After a couple of years the offers to move into other positions had dried up. He would occasionally be asked to cover for someone and half-heartedly asked if he would do it permanently, but with no real expectation that he was thinking of anything apart from getting back into the car park. At his last performance review Mr Barclay had told him that it was reassuring to know that the outside of the store was so well looked after and to keep up the good work. Tim took this as the compliment it was intended to be, then shrugged his Hi-Viz jacket back on and went back outside.

He started the day by doing a tour of all the likely places the trolleys could have ended up; sometimes the café used them to collect their consumables for the day, or the stock room grabbed them to put things in when the packaging had split. As he finished his unsuccessful hunt he went back to his corner of the delivery area to double check that he hadn't just overlooked them, although he knew he hadn't. When he got there he was not surprised to find that the two trolleys from the day before yesterday were still not there. What did surprise him was that neither was the one he had put there just last night.

Exasperated, he went to the front of the building to start his shift properly, mulling over what might or might not have happened to the trolleys and worrying about whether someone was having a joke with him. It wouldn't have been the first time that some of the younger lads had tried to tease him; he knew they thought he wasn't smart enough to realise. They were usually so wrapped up in their own brilliant coronas that they didn't look closely enough at other people to find out what they were like.

Of course, this wasn't all the inside staff. Some went out of their way to be nice to him. Sonia from the café had known him since he was a young boy, she always refilled his flask for him on cold days, and more than once he had found a cake left on his seat which he was certain she had smuggled out for him. Other staff were parents of children he and his brother had gone to school with; they were always polite to him. The younger staff tended to keep to themselves, he had occasionally been asked along to a night out, but the offers tend to dry up if you never take them up. There had even been one or two tentative invitations that Tim had been certain were intended to be dates. Although Tim didn't really think of himself as dating material he had been almost persuaded by Lisa with her long black hair and twin dimples that had appeared on her cheeks when she smiled out from under her fringe. But he had changed his mind at the last minute, letting her know before the end of her shift, so as not to stand her up. He knew he shouldn't be away from the house for too long, and the thought of talking to someone he didn't know made the muscles in his neck and shoulders twitch.

He quietly got on with his day, well, as quiet as you can be in a busy car park with a hundred unruly trolleys anyway. Today was one of the slightly quieter mornings of the week. The group of young mums in lycra, who visited the café after taking their assorted babies to the nearby swimming pool had been and gone. He was sure they spent longer drinking coffee than they did exercising – he guessed that was the point. Talking; animatedly to each other, busily to their phones and joyfully to their babies, as they made their busy way back to their homes. Soon the shuttle bus would arrive and disgorge a full load of pensioners into the waiting doors; by the time they had shuffled their way round it would be the end of the school day and parents with small children in bright red or royal blue (depending on which school they attended) sweatshirts would start to appear, to gather what was needed for the evening meal and provide snacks for those who had the after-school munchies.

Not long after them would come the teenagers, unaccompanied by adults and usually arriving in packs. They would load up with anything with a high sugar content that would help them survive the arduous journey back to their homes, pockets and backpacks full. Following them would be people returning from work, parking hurriedly and consulting lists on their phones as they dashed in to find whatever it was they had remembered – or been instructed – to collect on their way home.

There was a pattern to the days, a predictability that meant he rarely had to consult his watch to know whereabouts he was in the day.

As he toured the area, looking for strays, he was always alert to the possibility that someone may need his assistance. He was happy to lift a bag or two into a car boot or collect a trolley for someone less mobile. His endeavours were usually met with gratitude, sometimes with indifference and occasionally with disrespect. He had long since learned not to challenge drivers who were blocking other cars because they were 'just popping in quickly', or to be surprised that they left their trolleys obstructing the pathways in their careless and entitled haste, their particular brand of outright rudeness was an interaction he could happily live without. He merely waited for them to leave then cleared up after them.

Knowing the rhythm of the days meant he knew when would be a good time to take a break; his small chair in a sheltered alcove at the side of the building was shared with inside staff who were taking smoke breaks. This was the main time that he met them, although he seldom interacted with them, preferring to let them get on with their own gossip and catch-ups while he listened – to all intents and purposes invisible, which was how he kept abreast of what was happening inside the store. This is not to say he was rude or standoffish, he would happily talk if someone wanted to, but most people preferred to leave him alone and he was happy with that.

Once, when Mr Barclay had been away (he couldn't think of him as Steve, it seemed wrong somehow) a stand-in manager who was keen to make a name for himself in head office had appeared while he was sipping some tea from his thermos that Sonia had kindly filled for him.

"Where do you record your breaks?" he had demanded.

"I don't."

"Well how do I know you're not taking too long or that you're not just sitting here all day?"

"Because the trolleys are all where they should be."

"Yes, but we don't pay you just to hang around here smoking."

"I'm not smoking."

"Just do your job, or I'll have to put it on your record. I'm leaving a note for Steve to follow this up."

"Okay."

Tim was surprised when Mr Barclay made a special trip out into the car park on his return.

"Tim, I got a message about what happened last week, I know you're always here before your shift, I know you don't go until you're done and I know you work hard. Take your breaks when you want, and don't forget you're always welcome to use the inside staffroom."

"Okay, thanks."

Tim knew that Mr Barclay's mum had been friends with his own mother at one time and wondered if that had something to do with it, although he suspected he knew the real reason, the one that people didn't talk about. Anyway, that was an end to it, he took his breaks when he needed to (not inside though). Sonia provided him with hot and cold drinks when he asked for them and nobody bothered him. In return he made sure trolleys, baskets and rubbish did not accumulate in the parking area that might cause disruption to the customers shopping experience.

At the end of the afternoon he ventured inside, to the office. The enigma of the missing trolleys had been turning round and round in his mind, it just didn't make sense. Mr Barclay's assistant, Jo, greeted him through a mask of make-up that Tim thought excessive for someone who spent most of their day filing forms and answering the phone.

"Hello Tim, we don't see you here often, how are you?"

"Yeah, I'm alright. I just wanted to let Mr Barclay know that the broken trolleys have been going missing."

"Okay, did you want to tell him yourself or shall I pass the message on?" she reached for her notepad, ready to transcribe a message if necessary.

"No, it's okay, I'm sure it's nothing, it's just that I can't find the damaged trolleys that I put in their usual place to be collected. I'm sure it's nothing."

Jo smiled as she scribbled on her pad then repeated back what he had just told her.

"Oh, that sounds serious, I'll be sure to pass that on, was there anything else?"

"No, that was it, I'm sure it's not important."

He was already turning to leave as she thanked him, he was certain that she thought he was as daft as everyone else did. The note of sarcasm and condescension in her tone had been slight, but it was there. He wished he hadn't bothered coming in to the office now, but it was done and he hurried out towards the car park and the tail end of his shift.

Chapter 5
Dinner for One

Closing the front door behind him Tim called out, "I'm home."

The house replied with silence; he shrugged and went to the kitchen to make a cup of tea before he changed and settled for the evening. He made something to eat and sat at the table, the plate was loaded with food which he started to eat as he spoke.

"I went to see Mr Barclay about the trolleys. I spoke to Jo, you know, his secretary. Anyway, nobody seems particularly bothered about the missing trolleys. I mean, I know they're only the broken ones but I couldn't find them anywhere."

He ate some more then continued, "If it keeps happening we'll start to get short, then people will start to complain. I'm pretty sure everyone will care about trolleys going missing then. I know it's not loads and loads of them, but the less there are the harder it is to keep the bays at the entrance full."

Finishing the last of his meal, which he washed down with the last gulps from his glass of water, he wiped his mouth with the back of his hand and continued, "I don't know what to do, even if that Jo does pass on the message to Mr Barclay he won't do anything, he'll just say 'oh it's only a couple of trolleys, I'm sure they'll turn up'. But it's not right, I know where I put them and I know they're not at the store - I looked everywhere."

He got up and clattered his dishes into the sink along with the pans and scrubbed them clean.

"It's not like when people take them home then leave them for kids to play with in the street, they get collected by the van when they get reported. These are broken, nobody could easily take them anywhere, it just doesn't make sense."

He paced up and down the kitchen, thinking over what he had just said.

"It just doesn't make sense. Who steals trolleys that don't work? And when do they do it? They must come at night mustn't they? After the store is closed, so why doesn't the CCTV see them? Or maybe it does and they just couldn't care less, easier to not do anything I guess."

By now he was sitting in the lounge, the remote in his hand. He fiddled with it, turning it over, examining it without actually switching the telly on. Then he stopped and looked up, his usually placid face replaced with a determination that most of his colleagues wouldn't have noticed even if they had looked at him for long enough to see it.

Even though he had spent the evening talking about the enigma of the missing trolleys he knew that he hadn't been heard. Although Ian looked back at him from numerous photos around the house he wasn't actually here. The words had fallen into the empty house and been swallowed by the answering silence.

It had been raining all morning, the drizzly type of rain that sits on your hair and clothes making you feel wetter than you actually are. The sky was dark with portentous clouds billowing in over the roofs and treetops, daring people to venture outside their houses.

They had tried playing outdoors, but their identical track suits had quickly become damp, then wet, then sodden and lastly cold. The soaked and muddy clothes now lay on the kitchen floor, close to, but not next to, the washing machine.

Frustrated with the boys hanging around the house complaining about the weather and their boredom, their mum had ordered them to 'find something to do before I find something for you'. This invariably meant some form of tortuous housework or other, so the twins had made themselves scarce. By the time the sun put in a tentative appearance Tim was half way through making an Airfix model of a biplane that had been sitting untouched in his pile of possessions since their birthday.

Ian had wanted to go straight out on their bikes the moment the clouds broke, to make up for lost time, he told him he would catch up once he had finished the final touches to his project. Ian grumbled, but nevertheless took his bike and sped off towards the park where he hoped some of their other friends would start to emerge now the rain from earlier was just a memory.

Tim finished attaching the propeller to the fuselage of his plane with a big gobbet of glue and a sigh of relief then hurried out to his red bike, which was on its side in the front garden. He shook the raindrops off it and wiped the saddle as dry as he could with his sleeve then cycled the short distance to the park, down the alley, along the imaginatively named Park Road and through the ornate wrought iron gates.

Ignoring the signs requesting him to keep off the grass, he made a beeline for the corner of the park where football was permitted. Surrounded by large bushes and trees for climbing, this patch of scrubby grass was a magnet for the local boys. He could see Finley, Josh and Chubbs kicking a well-worn football between them as they waited for enough people to turn up to make two scratch teams and start a game. No Ian though. He looked about, saw a familiar bike over by the largest tree at the far edge of the area and cycled over to it.

He had expected to find Ian up the tree, watching to see who was arriving while he waited for Tim – he could hardly start playing without his teammate could he? Only he wasn't, nor was he behind the bushes or in the branches of any of the smaller trees.

He sat astride his bike, looking at Ian's abandoned bike laying on its side in the wet grass wondering where to look next when the football rolled over towards him. He looked to see Chubbs jogging over half-heartedly to collect it. When he got closer he called to him, "Chubbs, have you seen Ian?"

"Nah, I thought it was his bike. It was there like that when we got here." He indicated the other boys, so no point asking them then.

Tim cycled around the rest of the park, past the pond full of duckweed and non-working fountain, around the selection of swings, roundabouts and climbing frames and even dared to cut through the beautifully tended rose garden. He eventually ended up back where he started, without having caught sight of his twin.

"Have you seen him yet?"

"No, are you going to play or what?" answered Chubbs, holding up the football.

Deciding his brother was playing some hilarious prank, Ian was cross that he had not been included in whatever it was he was up to. He went and joined the football game which now had two teams of three, two other boys having turned up while he had been searching the park. He tried, but was distracted, with half an eye constantly scanning the dripping trees, looking out for Ian. Without his usual playing partner he played badly anyway, ending up standing between two coats where he let in goal after goal.

Some other boys turned up in dribs and drabs, until there were enough players for Tim to be able to slip away without upsetting the delicate balance of the game, which was finely poised at 13 – 15 (several of the goals were penalties that Chubbs had awarded himself – it was his ball.) He went home to see if Ian had gone there, although he couldn't think why he would have left his bike behind. Anyway, he wasn't and mum was busy. Tim cycled to the corner shop, where Mr Moore hadn't seen him, then back to the park.

Finally he returned home and asked Mum if she knew where Ian was. That was when things got really weird. Mum told him to stay indoors and went out, returning half an hour later and making Tim describe exactly what had happened – a story that Tim would tell so often over the coming weeks that it would become indelibly imprinted on his memory.

CHAPTER 6
Dinner for One (again)

Finally someone came to take over her till – it was Gavin, cutting it fine as usual. Wendy signed out of the register and slid off the vinyl stool, allowing Gavin to take over and start truculently serving the next customer in the queue. Her back and shoulders were aching and stiff as she walked to the staffroom to collect her coat and bag before going home.

On the way out she stopped by the fridge filled with ready-meals, selecting what to have for her evening meal. She knew she should really be in the fruit and veg aisles, planning a healthy meal for the evening, but preparing and cooking a meal from scratch always seemed such a hassle for one person. So she chose a microwave fish pie, picked up a bottle of wine and paid. She then went out of the shop, saying goodbye to various members of staff on her way.

She stepped into the fresh air. It was cool, a light wind stopping the heat of the sun from making an impression as it lowered in the sky. While she had been working the day had passed, the world outside had marched through its routine in her absence. The sun had travelled most of the way across the sky, the weather had changed its mind several times, people had come and gone and the hours and minutes had dissolved.

Crossing the car park to the bus stop she saw Tim arranging a line of trolleys into a semblance of orderliness as he prepared to return them to the front of the store, Trolley Tim, as he was affectionately known by the other staff. She passed right by him, pausing as she approached.

"Hi Tim, how's it going?"

Tim looked up, seemingly surprised that somebody had spoken to him.

"Hi, yeah, all good out here. How about you?"

"Glad to be going home, what time are you off?"

She didn't really need to ask, she knew that Tim would still be here at seven o'clock regardless of what his timesheet said. Only then would he finally be satisfied that he had done as much as he could to keep the carpark clutter free and ready for the next day. She liked Tim, he always had a nice smile and remembered who she was without having to look at her name badge. He seemed to enjoy what he did as well, so what if it was only doing the trolleys, someone had to do it, and he did it well.

"Another hour or so," replied Tim, "have a nice evening."

"Will do, you too."

She left it at that and continued on her way, mentally planning her evening as she walked. Not that there was much to plan. It would follow a similar pattern to most evenings that she wasn't on duty as a special constable. She would go home and change out of her supermarket uniform and put on her running gear. She hadn't been much of one for physical activity before she had applied to the force; it had come as a twofold surprise to her that they had such stringent requirements for joining, regarding health, and that her own fitness levels had dipped so alarmingly since leaving behind the compulsory PE lessons of secondary school.

She had found it hard at first, but had persevered and found that her ability and stamina had gradually increased and, to her surprise, that she had actually come to enjoy it. Her evening run had gradually increased in length (although staying at roughly the same amount of time) and when she missed it for some reason she felt restless.

After that was complete she would have her evening meal, catch up with any chores that needed doing, make sure that everything was ready for the following day and check her emails and phone messages. Finally she would settle down with a mug of tea and multi-task between watching TV and reading the manuals she had been provided with that contained all the information that aspiring police officers needed to be familiar with.

Occasionally she would have a stilted and awkward conversation with her mum over the phone. Not that they didn't get on, but her mum still didn't understand why Wendy had moved hundreds of miles away, to a different part of the country. She took it very personally indeed. It didn't matter how often Wendy tried to explain how important it had been for her to escape from the toxic group of friends that she had gone to school with, her mum just didn't get it.

The friends had all gone through school together, Trish, Mish, Carol and Wendy. You would rarely see one of them without one or more of the others in tow, from the age of twelve when they were all allocated the same tutor group at secondary school. They were well matched intellectually and had similar interests, sharing the same passions, crushes, bands and fashions. They weren't exclusive, other girls were very much part of their social circle. They weren't unkind, there was no bullying or teasing of less outgoing or more bookish girls. But they were tight knit, confiding in one another and trusting each other.

As they progressed through school and puberty took hold they started to mature and change, gradually growing into the bodies that were the fledgling forms of the adults they would become. And Wendy was bigger than the others, not taller and not fatter, just bigger. This wasn't a problem until, at the age of 14, Mish decided she needed to go on a diet. Sharing pictures of models from Cosmopolitan, she explained to the others how she wanted to look in six months' time – waspish waist, prominent boobs held on slender ribs and shoulders with stick-like arms and legs. For the first time Wendy became aware of her own body's failures and shortcomings.

Thus started the 'year of not eating'. For the others it was intermittent, fasting one day then not so much the next because it was chips at lunchtime or they fancied a day off and they'd earnt it. But for Wendy, as the year progressed, it became a serious business – deadly serious. She would go for days with barely any food, then binge, vomit and start over.

As the weight started to drop off there was a time when she flaunted her tight-fitting clothes when she was with her friends, finally able to compare herself equally to them. Of course, she continued to get smaller, more fragile and began to cover up with looser, baggier clothes so people wouldn't comment. Her periods stopped, which was a mixture of relief from the inconvenience of them, and a sense of loss for something that she had only recently started to get used to.

Things came to a head when she fainted in PE. There was a great deal of concern and worry once everybody had realised what had been going on, followed by a long and protracted recovery. If that had been the only thing, Wendy could have forgiven her friends, but it wasn't.

There had been the afternoon that Carol had produced a bottle of Cinzano from her mother's drink cabinet. The afternoon of underage boozing had culminated in Wendy throwing up in the precinct and getting a ride home in a police car after her friends had left her on her own, wandering off to steal some make up from a nearby store.

Then there was the occasion that she had given her virginity to Tom Bailey, convinced that the other girls had already had sex with their own boyfriends. Their horrified response, followed by their insistence on knowing all the details, quickly helped her realise that they had been encouraging her to try it as a test run for their own yet to come sexual adventures.

In the end, leaving town seemed the logical thing to do. To break away from the small-town mentality and unchanging, unable to change, friends that she had grown up with who had no intention of moving on and were always happy to let her take the fall.

So here she was, sitting in her fleece pyjamas with the obligatory mug of tea beside her, Blackstone's 'Preparing for Police Duty' open on her lap and the news on the TV - enjoying an evening with no cares or worries beyond remembering to switch on her alarm before she went to sleep.

CHAPTER 7
Bandits

The lady in the blue dress was obviously having some difficulty. She had managed to get from the checkout to the main door, but was now standing behind the wheelchair gently singing to the agitated boy who was slowly starting to calm, responding to the strains of a long forgotten nursery rhyme. As she sang the lady picked her bags up again and tried to hang them back on the handles of the chair.

Again, the boy objected, pushing them back off so they had to be caught before they crashed to the floor. The lady looked as if she was at her wit's end.

"Come on Noah, it's only as far as the car. You let me do it last time."

He was clearly having none of it, wanting nothing to interfere with his personal space, even if it was the food he had just chosen with his mum inside the shop. The bags were now on the floor again, and Noah grinned hugely and fluttered his hands in front of himself. A frown appeared on his mum's face and her own hands swam as she spoke again.

"No, it's not funny. We need to get to the car or we won't be able to go home."

Other people passed by on their way in and out of the shop. Some ignored them completely, others stared at what was going on. One woman tutted and shook her head as she walked past, muttering under her breath.

Tim had seen enough. He walked across the short distance to them and asked if they needed a hand. His question surprised the woman who looked up at him as she once again bent to sing to the boy, who was content again now that the bags had been removed once more. The look of relief on her face was clear as she straightened up.

"Yes please, if you could, I would really appreciate it. I don't know what's got into him today. Could you watch our bags while I get him into the car?"

"I'll carry them over for you," he said, moving forward to take the handles of the bags.

"Really, you don't need to. I don't want to make extra work for you."

"It's not a problem, I was going over that way anyway to clear the trolleys." As he said it he realised that he didn't know which way they would actually be going, he had not seen them arrive. The lady didn't seem to notice his gaffe.

"That would be lovely if you don't mind, I'm really sorry we're all the way over there," she pointed to the far edge of the car park, "there were no disabled bays left."

"Lead on," said Tim as he picked up the bags and started to walk alongside them in the direction of a large blue Chrysler.

The boy's hands waved and his mum bent forward, paused, then brushed her hair back from her face as she straightened up.

"Yes, the man is helping, and no, it's definitely not funny Noah."

This admonishment was given with a kind smile that Noah returned, he then looked around at Tim and with an even bigger gap-toothed smile made some more signs.

"He says hello. He wants to know your name."

"Hello to you," Tim started to say to the mum, before correcting himself and looking back towards Noah, "my name's Tim."

This elicited a broad grin and a proffered hand, presumably to shake. Tim was unable to oblige as his own hands were occupied by the bags. As they arrived at the car he placed the bags on the ground and offered his own hand, which was taken and shaken with enthusiasm.

"Thank you so much," said Noah's mum, "that was really kind of you."

"It was no trouble at all, nice to meet you, Noah."

This last earned him another smile, a second handshake and some more rapid signs that he needed the mum to interpret for him.

"He's saying 'thank you for helping – and goodbye'. Really thank you, Tim, it was very kind of you."

"Not at all, you have a good day."

He went over to collect two trolleys from nearby, to back up his cover story. As he returned Noah was settled in the car, still waving goodbye, and the wheelchair and bags had been safely stowed. Noah's mum smiled and thanked him again as he passed, she looked relieved to have finished this part of her day. Tim wondered how much patience she must have. However much it was, she looked as if she would need it to get through the rest of the afternoon and evening.

He made his way to the front of the shop, collecting trolleys as he went, and scanning the faces of the people who were coming and going. As he was placing his load into its correct slot there was a commotion behind him, shouting and a colourful flurry of movement that compelled him to turn around and look, to see what was going on. What was going on was a group of five teenagers running out of the shop, dodging past the other customers and splitting up to run across to the various egress points around the edges of the store's area. Not the official ones of course, the gaps in hedges and low fences that led directly to the maze of alleys and backstreets on the neighbouring housing estate.

Behind them came Ahmed – a long way behind.

"Stop them! Stop those kids!"

It was a hopeless request as the kids were already out of reach of anybody, even if they had been prepared to have a try at holding on to them. Ahmed clearly knew this, he stopped in the doorway with his hands on his hips and watched as the last kid sat on the top of the fence and extended his middle finger of his right hand before disappearing from view.

"You okay?" asked Tim.

"Yeah, those bloody kids again. They sneak in when I'm not looking, I swear I'll catch them one day."

Those *'bloody kids'* were the *'pick'n'mix bandits'* as the staff had come to call them. Every so often they would descend on the store and make their way around, cheerfully eating anything and everything they could on the way; doughnuts, sweets, crisps, peanut butter - helping themselves to the smorgasbord on offer while evading staff. They would then run and scatter as they had done now.

"I'm going to catch them one day, then we'll see who's laughing."

Tim knew Ahmed had grainy pictures of the pick'n'mix bandits, taken from the CCTV cameras, taped to the inside of his podium by the front door of the shop.

"Well, not today, Ahmed. Take it easy, I'll keep an eye out for them and let you know if I see them coming."

"Thanks, Tim." Ahmed looked irritated still, he would now have to go inside, assess what damage they had done and write a report about it. Tim was glad that his trolleys didn't give him that sort of headache, apart from the ones that had gone missing that is.

CHAPTER 8
....or Get Off the Pot

The trolleys still bothered him, the only possible explanation he could think of was that someone was taking them in the night. Which was ridiculous of course, who would want a broken trolley? Who would want several broken trolleys? It just didn't make sense. The more he dwelt on it the more it bothered him.

He wondered what Ian would say if he was here. Actually he didn't, he knew full well.

That summer Ian had learnt a new phrase that had delighted him - 'shit or get off the pot.' He had used it at any and every opportunity, apart from when their mum or dad were in earshot. It suited his impatient nature, he was always the one who wanted to be onto the next thing; people to see, places to go. Mum always said it was why he was born first – 47 whole minutes! It was probably also why he had not been able to wait for Tim that afternoon.

Mum had come back from the park 15 minutes after she had left the house, wheeling Ian's bike beside her. She asked several times, in several different ways, if Tim knew where Ian had gone or where he was likely to be.

When he was unable to provide any kind of useful or helpful answer to his increasingly cross mum, Tim was sent back to the park to 'have a really good look' while mum got out her address book and started calling the parents of other kids that we used to play with.

He cycled round the park three times, looking in bushes and up trees as he passed them, then returned home once more. When he got back his dad was waiting by the front door, which was odd as it was ages before the time he usually arrived home. His dad took him straight back to the park and made Tim show him the exact spot that the bike had been laying; the football boys had all left now and there was no sign that anybody had ever been there at all – apart from some crisp packets and a single raincoat goalpost, which meant someone was going to be for it. They then walked around the park with Tim pointing out all the spots that he used to frequent with his brother.

Mum was waiting expectantly on the front doorstep; from the corner of his eye Tim saw his dad shake his head and mum disappeared inside before they got to the door. As he approached he heard her voice, "Yes, police please, I'd like to report a missing person."

Dad ushered him upstairs as they went in, telling him to "Go and make something with your Lego, I'll come and see you in a bit."

Tim wanted to remind him that the Lego was really Ian's thing, but decided that now probably wasn't the time. He went up and carried on where he had left off with his model plane while trying to listen to what was going on downstairs.

He didn't have to wait too long to find out. From his bedroom window he saw a police car park a little way along the road. A tall blond policeman got out, checked his notebook and looked towards their house before walking unhurriedly up to the front door. Tim crept onto the landing to try and hear what was being said, but they vanished into the kitchen before he could make anything out.

Again, it was only a short time before he was summoned downstairs and asked to tell the tall policeman, now sitting at the kitchen table with a mug of tea, exactly what had happened that afternoon. He told him, trying not to leave out anything. He wrote down some of the details in a notebook while Tim spoke, interjecting occasionally with questions.

Why didn't Tim go with Ian? Tim wondered this himself now and wished, not for the last time, that he had. Why did Tim play football instead of coming back and telling someone? He had no satisfactory answer but the questions would keep asking themselves in his head for years to come.

The policeman excused himself and went into the kitchen to talk on his radio, he still sounded unhurried and relaxed. Tim was told he could go back upstairs if he wanted, it was not really an optional thing. As he went up the stairs he could hear the policeman's voice.

"Hi control, we've got a missing child here. Could we put all units on alert for..."

The door closed and Tim returned to his room, realising too late that he was hungry. He would have to rely on the stash of sweets that he and Ian kept in the wardrobe to keep him going for a bit. He was sure that Ian would understand if he ate some of his share, after all it was his fault that Tim was stuck here.

The minutes dragged into an hour before Tim was distracted from his book by a wash of intermittent blue light that came through his window. Looking out he saw that a second police car had arrived; it was parked directly outside this time and two more police officers came to the house – a man and a lady. Tim waited for them to come in and started to make his way downstairs hoping to sneak past the distracted adults and find something to eat in the kitchen.

No such luck. Dad had been on his way to collect him anyway and intercepted him on the stairs.

"Tim, there's somebody else who needs to talk to you."

"Okay, can I have something to eat?"

"Yes, in a minute. Can you talk to the police lady first?"

Tim did. It was all the same questions as previously and more; where did Tim think Ian could be? Who were their friends? Had he talked about running away? Was he unhappy? It went on and on, the only simple part were the questions about what he looked like and what he was wearing – identical meant exactly what it said on the box.

Tim was then driven in the police car, with all the neighbours watching him get in, to the park. They drove right in and across the grass to the unofficial football pitch where Tim showed them exactly *where he had found Ian's bike. He knew the exact spot even though it was now nearly dark.*

He was then returned home, where yet another police car had arrived, and was taken back indoors. His mum hugged him, held him tightly, then made him a sandwich. He was told he could go to bed if he wanted, nobody could answer his question about where Ian was, although the police lady – who had told him to call her Kath – was very kind and explained that they were doing everything they could and that everybody was looking for Ian, she was sure they would find him soon.

Suitably reassured, Tim went upstairs to bed where he lay awake most of the night looking at Ian's empty bed and wishing he had gone with him when it had stopped raining.

So, shit or get off the pot. Tim gathered his flask and his coat, put some crisps in his pocket and went back to the supermarket, where he arrived just after they had finished locking up for the night. There would be night staff inside of course, restocking and restacking the shelves, but nobody would be using the front entrance or the car park now until 6.30 when everything would start anew.

He settled onto his break chair, adjusting it slightly so he would have a better view of the entrance, then he waited.

And he waited.

And he waited.

Tim was good at waiting. He started to doze a couple of times, taking a sip of coffee or standing up and stretching when he felt this happening. He watched Orion move slowly across the sky. He listened to the sound of the traffic, slowly dwindling to intermittent cars out on some lonely mission. In the distance a siren sounded briefly and a church bell introduced each new hour as it arrived.

By three thirty he had decided that the damaged cart he had put aside that afternoon was probably safe for the night. It was full dark with only a sliver of moon. The lights from the supermarket lit the front of the store, making sure passers-by could see the name even if they couldn't visit right now. Soon the overnight delivery lorries would start to arrive and the building would start to wake from its slumber.

Just as he had decided to go home and get a little sleep himself, a car came into the car park. Headlights on full beam, it drove around the edge of the area, driving towards the corner which was a dead spot for the CCTV. He watched as it came to a halt and switched off its headlights. Surely this wouldn't be the trolley thief? You would have a job fitting a trolley into a BMW 3 series. He sat still, waiting to see what would happen.

He did not have to wait long. A second car, a Land Rover Defender, arrived. It followed the same route as the first car, pulling up alongside it and stopping. Tim waited, stock still, to see what would happen. You could definitely fit a trolley into this car, but why would they both need to be here?

Two figures got out of their respective cars; it was hard to tell if they were male or female from this distance. The Land Rover driver opened the back of his car and took out a small box, the other shadowy person looked inside it briefly then took something from his pocket which he exchanged for the box. Something was said between the two of them, then they returned to their cars and left, driving off into the night, leaving Tim with more questions than answers.

CHAPTER 9
A Night Out

Wendy was back in the car with Mark, on their way to their evening's assignment. At the station there had seemed to be more people than usual, some she recognised, others who had clearly been co-opted from other stations temporarily to provide extra cover.

There was some information about what was going on; an elderly couple had been brutally attacked in their own home, an ordinary semi-detached house in a quiet side street near the centre of town. They were both in hospital; the man was now in recovery, but it was unsure if his wife would make it through the night.

Mark had given her a more detailed explanation once they were in the car. Rather than a burglary gone wrong, which was what had been widely assumed so far, it seemed to be a dazzlingly incompetent, drug related, gang hit on completely the wrong house. The attackers had been so infuriated not to find the people they had been looking for, or the crop of cannabis plants, that the couple had been beaten in the hope that they would give up the location of the actual drug house. Of course they couldn't, which had only made the attack more frenzied.

Extra resources had been pulled in to help with door to door enquiries, extra patrols to reassure the public, interviews with people known to be, or suspected of being, part of the local drug scene. Also, to execute warrants on those same people if they decided they didn't want to be interviewed. This was high-profile and all the stops had been pulled to try and get a quick result.

"So where are we going?" Wendy asked.

"We have the pleasure of the most glamourous, exciting and high profile aspect of police work this evening."

"Which is?"

"Wait and see."

And that was how Wendy came to be standing outside an ordinary looking semi-detached house in a quiet street for the rest of the evening. Their job was to not let anybody into the house until forensics had finished photography, dusting and collating everything. Screens had been put up at the windows to stop people looking in, occasionally a white clad figure would emerge from the dazzlingly bright light coming out of the front door to deposit a plastic bag in the van parked on the driveway or to speak to a detective who was eager to get back inside the house.

Mostly though, the job involved being photographed by the press and telling them that neither she nor Mark had any comment to make. Saying the same thing to small gaggles of concerned locals who approached them and waving away small boys on BMX bikes who circled like prepubescent vultures. Eventually the cameras started to drift away and the remaining newsmen hung around on the other side of the road, not really expecting anything else to happen but waiting just in case. One of them, a seasoned local reporter introduced herself to them as 'JoTurnberryfromtheEcho' - as if it was all one word, and managed to get them some coffee from somewhere.

"It won't get any more information from us you know?" Mark smiled.

"I know that, but you looked like you needed some. And maybe you'll remember me if you do have anything extra or interesting that you can share."

"We'll be sure to keep you in mind."

"Also, if there's anything I can do to help you."

"Such as?"

"Who knows? It can't hurt to cooperate with each other can it?"

Anyway, she was right about Wendy needing the coffee, it had been a long night. It carried on for some time, with the forensics team eventually clearing out and heading back to their labs at about one in the morning. A detective followed them out and closed the door, the remaining press immediately came across to him as he walked down the path, intercepting him next to Mark and Wendy and bombarding him with questions.

He held his hand up for silence, then spoke to them,

"I can only tell you what you already know, this was a very serious assault on a couple in their own home and we are doing everything we can to find and apprehend the assailants. There will be a press conference tomorrow at nine, until then go home, write your draft copy and get some sleep."

Surprisingly, they did what they were told. Wendy guessed that they would be back in force tomorrow morning and was glad she wouldn't be having her photo taken over and over again at the press conference. Tonight was bad enough. The reporters started to move off, the detective stayed, waiting for them to go, then spoke to Mark.

"Thank you, you did a good job this evening. Both of you."

He nodded towards Wendy.

"It's the less exciting part of the job, but it's really important. People need to see someone approachable, as well as a thug like Mark."

"Are you saying she's prettier than me?" asked Mark, and they both laughed at what was clearly an ongoing joke between the two of them.

"Seriously though, what's your name?"

"Wendy."

"Well stick around him, Wendy, he knows what he's doing. Anyway, the guys are coming to secure the house soon, I'd like you to stay here until someone comes to take over from you, make sure the neighbours know we haven't abandoned them tonight, okay?"

"That's fine, we'll hold on here. I'll look threatening and Wendy can look approachable."

They both laughed again, and Wendy joined them this time. Then the detective bid them goodnight, went to his car and left, presumably to get some sleep before what was clearly going to be a busy day.

The locksmith came with his bag of tools and made sure the house was locked up tight, he passed the keys to Mark before he left, and then Wendy and Mark were alone.

"You know what this was all about don't you?" he asked.

"Arguing over their patches?"

"No, not just that. There are new drugs coming in, nobody is sure where from but it's upsetting the balance of things. It's annoying our bosses too because we can't figure out how to stop them. We had a fairly good idea before about how things worked and we could disrupt it if and when we needed to. Whenever we tried to stop it, it just shifted the problem. It was always about damage limitation really. But now…well now things have changed, so we need to figure out what we need to do to change as well."

"So nobody has any idea where the new supplies are coming from?"

"There are theories, everybody and his brother has got an idea about it. They all agree that no big shipments are coming in, it's all arriving a bit at a time. It wouldn't make sense to be driving it all down from the cities one tiny shipment at a time. Besides, all the players in the cities are under surveillance, and they're not going anywhere."

"So they're bringing it another way?"

"Looks like it."

"Could they be posting it?"

"Someone thought of that, they've had the dog unit at the sorting depot for weeks and got nothing."

"The train."

"Again, nobody thinks it's likely they would do something that public – too risky. However they're doing it, it's successful."

"So how….no, never mind."

"Go on, there's no stupid questions."

"Yeah, only stupid people, I know." They both laugh at this, then Wendy continued, "Well, if it's a new set up surely it's just a matter of time before we catch up?"

"I hope so, people are getting hurt." He indicated the house behind them.

"Won't the other regular dealers know?"

"They've been squeezed, but apparently not. They're too busy blaming each other at the moment."

They both paused, the absence of their conversation leaving a soundless vacuum in the still, dark night. A dog barked in the distance, just as Mark was radioing in to let control know that all was quiet at the house. The conversation turned to Wendy's application to join the force full time. Mark was encouraging and positive, telling her he would rather patrol with her than some of the other numpties he had worked with over the years.

"Listen," he told her, "it can be hard sometimes, especially for women. They only started letting unmarried mothers stay on in the force recently."

"Really?"

"Really, some of the lads don't get the line between banter and being offensive and most people aren't going to put their own neck on the line to stick up for you."

"I've noticed," Wendy grimaced.

"What I'm saying is, don't let it get you down, and don't take any nonsense – give as good as you get."

"Are you telling me to toughen up?" she smiled in his direction.

"Kind of, just be yourself, you're already tough."

"Am I?"

"You've got this far haven't you?"

"I suppose."

"And don't forget, just because people don't offer help doesn't mean you can't ask for it. In my experience mostly that's what they're waiting for."

"I'll remember that, thanks, Mark."

They reverted to silence for a few moments, then Mark asked, "Did you see the match yesterday?"

"What match?"

"Oh my, you don't stand a chance, they'll eat you alive."

They both laughed and she punched him lightly on the arm as the relief car pulled up.

"Is she assaulting you?" asked the relief as Mark handed over the keys.

"No, she was just pissed off because her team lost last night. Isn't that right?" he asked Wendy.

"If you say so, come on let's get back and finish off our shift. I want to turn in now."

"Have a nice night then you two," the relief smiled, winking at Mark.

"I will, once I'm tucked up in bed with the missus. See you."

The car was warm after the cool of the night and they sat in companiable silence on their way back to the station. Wendy was glad she had an ally at least, she got the idea that she might need at least one in the coming months.

CHAPTER 10
A Different Night Out

T he following day was a quiet one for Tim, he spent much of it thinking about what he had seen the previous night. He was pretty sure about what it was that he witnessed, but had no real proof so he couldn't really take it to anyone. It bothered him, not knowing what to do, and he decided he needed to sleep on it while he made his mind up about what he needed to do next.

After drifting, preoccupied, through the day, he went into the store at the end of his shift to do his own shopping. Some ready meals plus some fruit and veg to balance them out. Some tea bags, coffee and milk then went to the sweet aisle for his usual; some Monster Munch, a large bag of Haribo and two Sherbert Fountains.

This part of his shop was always the same, it was a recreation of the stash that he and Ian had accrued in their room. He had finished most of it that first week, when meals had been unpredictable in their frequency, timing and quality. More often than not he had been making himself sandwiches in the kitchen in the moments when nobody else was around. Now he replenished the same items regularly, making sure the stash was always full.

Returning home he unpacked the shopping, taking the sweets upstairs and putting them in the bottom drawer of the chest of drawers, as was his habit. Then he made himself a mug of tea and a perfunctory meal, sitting at the table and calling loudly to the next room.

"I think they were drug dealers, you know, but I didn't really see them, or their car number plates. One of them was tall with long hair, the other was shorter and was wearing a long coat. I think the short one had a dog in his Land Rover. But that's the best I could see, it was dark and they were on the other side of the car park."

He finished his mug of tea and retrieved his jacket potato with his hand wrapped in a double-folded tea towel. He covered it with butter and cheese before setting it on the table and continuing to talk between mouthfuls.

"I don't know what to do, the police won't do anything because I didn't really see anything. Except I did, I just didn't see enough to get any details. I think I'll go back again tonight, see if they come again. I'm not staying all night again though, I'll set my alarm and go over just before they get there. Assuming they come at the same time, who knows? It won't hurt to look and see, will it?"

He knew it would be all about the waiting in the end, if he wanted to get to the bottom of what he had seen. He knew about waiting.

The following weeks had been hard, and slightly surreal. There had been police officers in the house most of the time, day and night. He had retold his own story a hundred times, until he could recite it by heart the moment someone asked. The park had been thoroughly searched, then the surrounding gardens, sheds, car parks, bins behind shops, even the empty school had been unlocked for them to hunt through the buildings. As if Ian would have gone into school in the summer holiday!

In spite of this, there was no sign of him. The newspapers had become involved as the police had appealed to the wider public for any information, having got nothing from their door to door enquiries in the local streets.

The story had rapidly escalated to become national news, Tim seeing his own face staring back at him from the front of the daily newspapers. It had been on the TV too, half of his school photo being flashed up for the whole world to see, encouraging everybody to look for Ian. But it felt like nobody was looking for Tim. His dad came into his room one night, swaying and slurring slightly, to tell Tim how much he loved him. His mum just burst into tears every time she saw him.

It wasn't as if he had any way of getting away from it either, he was well and truly trapped in the house. As long as Ian was missing there was no chance at all that he would be allowed out to play. The hardest part was that nobody had really asked him how he was doing, apart from the nice policeman called Jim. He had been at the house regularly and always found time to talk to Tim when he could, which was fairly regularly as there really wasn't that much he could do at the house apart from be there.

Two weeks after Ian had vanished, and one week before the start of school – which in spite of himself, Ian was actually looking forward to now – Carol came to see him in his bedroom.

"Tim, I need to ask you if you'll do something for us, for Ian."

"What is it?"

"We'd like to film you cycling to the park, just like Ian did. It will go on telly and might help people remember if they saw anything."

"Why wouldn't they remember?"

"Well sometimes people don't, then when they see it on TV it reminds them."

"Will it help find Ian?"

"It might do. We hope so."

"Okay, come on then."

He picked up his shoes and started to put them on; Carol laughed in spite of herself.

"Sorry, I should have said, not right now. We'll do it tomorrow when the cameras are here. You'll need to wear the same clothes as he was wearing and ride his bike. It will be at the same time of day as when Ian went out."

"Oh, okay. I'm not really supposed to ride Ian's bike though."

"I think everyone will make an exception this one time."

So the next day Tim was wearing his version of Ian's outfit, standing astride Ian's bike outside the house while various TV cameras and photographers bustled around getting everything ready. Tim had imagined it would be one man with a camera, the sheer volume of people involved had amazed him. Carol had stayed by his side the whole time, and mum had come over, given him a hug and a kiss and told him what a good boy he was. She had been crying, and looked as though she was about to again. As a photographer took a photo of her embracing her remaining son she burst into tears and rushed back into the house.

"C'mon guys," Carol entreated the photographers, "back off a bit, give them some space will you?"

The man who had taken the photo shrugged and merged back into the melee of other press reporters. Then it was time.

Tim rode the short distance to the park, cycling across the grass and ending up in the place he had found Ian's bike, where he laid the borrowed bike on its side then looked at the film crew, waiting for them to tell him what to do next. Which, of course, was the problem. Carol came over to him and started to walk him home, she had a Mars bar in her pocket that she passed to him.

"You did great, you were really brave. Well done."

Tim didn't feel brave, every slow turn of the pedals had felt like treachery. Ian wouldn't have ridden like this, he would have cycled as fast as he could, always in a hurry to get wherever he was going. In spite of the people around him Tim felt alone and wondered if Ian felt the same. As he approached the trees he tried to imagine what it was that his brother had seen that had made him leave his bike on the wet grass and vanish into thin air.

"Will that be on TV now?"

Silly question, it was on every news bulletin on every channel. It was on Crimewatch, it was on a special programme that had been hastily *assembled about missing children. It was on ad-infinitum, so much so that Tim stopped watching TV because he was fed up of seeing himself riding Ian's bike to the park.*

But it didn't help find Ian. It didn't jog anybody's memory into revealing information that would lead to him. There were various reports of mysterious vans, strangers seen nearby, theories about organised gangs kidnapping children and murmurings about UFO abductions. But nothing that was actually useful.

The alarm clock rang at the allotted time and Tim made his way to the car park, where he stood waiting in the dark until it started to rain. No cars had arrived and nothing else had happened, apart from some rats that had scurried along the side of the building, lit up by the light high on the corner of the shop. Tim made a mental note to let the maintenance guys know that he had seen them so that they could refresh the traps. He didn't see any reason to let them know when he had seen the rats, he didn't want to explain why he had been in the car park in the early hours of the morning. He went home and went back to bed.

CHAPTER 11

A Brief Encounter

Wendy had sighed deeply when she found that it was Gavin who was due to take over from her again, bracing herself for another last minute rush when he decided to saunter into work. Instead he had surprised her by turning up a couple of minutes early. She sorted herself out and made her way out of the shop towards the bus stop.

Halfway across the car park she saw Tim, he was holding a trolley for an elderly man, patiently waiting while he folded his walking frame into the back of the car. 'If only there was a bit more of that in the world' she thought as she went on her way.

She hadn't got far when she noticed rapid footsteps behind her, turning she saw Tim hurrying towards her. She stopped and waited while he caught up.

"Hi Wendy, how are you?"

"I'm fine thanks, and you?"

"Yeah, all good. Uhm, I know this is a silly question, but are you a police officer?"

"A special constable, yes, does it show?"

"No, I thought I'd seen you in town once, when I went out for chips."

She knew he had, she had seen him too, it had taken her a moment to recognise him in his non-work clothes. No fluorescent yellow jacket or woolly hat, but jeans and a t-shirt with his hair hanging loose on his shoulders instead of tied back. She had thought he looked kind of cute, in a vulnerable, shy way. Which was in contrast to some of the brash extroverts she had dated in the past.

"Well yes, that was probably me. Why do you ask?"

"This is going to sound silly – no, it is silly, it's okay, forget it."

"No come on, you can't leave me hanging like that, what is it?"

"I think someone's stealing the broken trolleys." He explained what had been going on and finished with, "I know it's not really serious, that's why I didn't go to the police – but it's bothering me."

Wendy didn't know whether it was serious or not, theft is theft after all. But there were certainly more consequential things to deal with.

"I can ask at the station, see if a car can come by occasionally, see if they see anything. I don't know what else we could do really."

She liked Tim's earnestness, the fact that he took his job seriously and that he seemed kind and helpful. What she had first mistaken for painful shyness she was realising was just someone who wanted to keep himself to himself, a private person. He seemed appreciative of her offer to mention it and thanked her, he looked as if he was on the brink of telling her something else, but instead he excused himself and left to retrieve and rehome some more trolleys.

CHAPTER 12
Making a Purchase

"I told the police about the trolleys today, I figured if Mr Barclay didn't want to do anything maybe they would. Well, I say 'the police', actually it was Wendy, she's a part-time policewoman. Anyway, she said she'd have a word at the station and see if they could drive by every so often."

He came back into the kitchen and finished making his mug of tea, then put the milk away and picked up a packet of digestives from the counter. He carried them both to the table and started dunking his first biscuit as he raised his voice towards the open kitchen door.

"I didn't say anything about the other thing, the men in the cars. They didn't come last night so I'm wondering if it was just a one off or if they only come on Monday nights or something like that."

As he spoke he steered the biscuit quickly towards his mouth, trying to beat the drop. He was successful, eating the biscuit with a sense of satisfaction out of proportion with the task accomplished. The next biscuit was already in transit to the cup.

"I don't know what I would have said anyway, it's not like I could tell them anything useful. It was dark and they were too far away for me to see what they looked like or the number plates on the cars, it wouldn't be a lot to go on would it?"

The second biscuit was safely consumed.

"What I need is something that I can…" he tailed off, ate another biscuit, paused thoughtfully, then continued, "I know, I'll get a video camera, then I can zoom in and film it next time it happens, that's what I'll do."

Ian loved gadgets, anything with a button or switch was like a magnet for him. Tim couldn't always see what the attraction was, he was interested – just not as enthusiastically as his brother.

On Ian's side of the room was a large music machine with a CD player, radio and double cassette deck. It had been his pride and joy when he had got it for Christmas that year, making tapes of his favourite songs for everybody and anybody that he knew, seeing how loud he could push the sonic boundaries in the house – then listening into the night with a pair of headphones he had saved his birthday money for.

Of course, Tim used it too, they shared everything. The pair of them rarely fell out over what belonged to who – everything was 'theirs'. That's not to say they didn't fall out, there were disagreements over who washed and who dried the dishes, whose turn it was to take the bins down and who was responsible for the mess in their bedroom.

Now there was only Tim in the bedroom, Ian's belongings waiting patiently for him to return. Tim spent a lot of time listening to the various mixtapes that Ian had produced, using the headphones to block out the various sounds from around the house; the crying, prolonged telephone calls and meetings with the police and arguments about what mum and dad both thought they should or shouldn't be doing.

For long periods of time he was forgotten, everybody's attention being focussed on where Ian might be and what they could do to locate him. He wished more than he had ever wished for anything that he had gone with his brother that day, sometimes even wishing that he had gone instead of Ian. When they remembered he was there his parents tried to reassure him that everything would be alright, but without any conviction themselves they did little to comfort him.

Going back to school had been hard. Ian's face was still featuring regularly in the news, with suggestions about what might have happened or speculation around the circumstances of his disappearance. Alongside his television appearance as Ian's stand-in Tim was a celebrity by default and the other kids didn't really know how to talk to him. Should they mention Ian or should they not? Would he still want to do the same things as before? Did they need to treat him differently? The teachers were in the same predicament, and they definitely did treat him differently, cutting him slack on his homework, not being harsh when he broke the rules – which he did with increasing regularity, especially now it appeared he could get away with it.

But it was at home that things were worst. He was virtually a prisoner in the house, having to be accompanied wherever he went and continuously running the gauntlet of photographers and reporters who hovered around hoping for a scoop, or at least a nugget of a story they could print.

As the weeks turned into months without any sign of Tim the story started to dwindle, so too did the quality of his home life. Mealtimes became hit and miss, he frequently had to forage in the kitchen to find something he could make for himself with his limited cooking capabilities. Dad seemed to be in the pub more and more now, while mum would take some of the tablets that the doctor had given her then retreat to her bedroom. When they were together the increasing tension became palpable, often ensuing in arguments that reverberated around the home. The resulting outpouring of affection that came in his direction after one of these was not enough to offset the depths of his fear and grief that he was left alone with every night.

Finally the police visits dwindled to nearly nothing, as they had nothing new to tell. Tim came home from school one evening and dad wasn't in (he was allowed to walk home alone again by now, the danger being perceived as past), he didn't come back that night. Or the next, or the next. When he did eventually reappear it was to collect a suitcase of belongings. He hugged Tim and kissed his forehead.

"Sorry Tim, it's just too hard to carry on like this."

Then he was gone. He communicated via birthday and Christmas cards for a couple of years, although birthdays and Christmas were not the magical events they had once been anymore. A place was always set at the table for Ian, creating a sombre, unhappy tone to *the festivities. Eventually they stopped doing this, but by then the potential for enjoying those celebrations had been lost.*

It was a beautiful spring day when Tim came home from school to find mum crying. In her hand she held a letter that she passed wordlessly to Tim before going back up to bed. Tim dispassionately read the news that his dad had died the previous week, dad had become a stranger and had abandoned them after all.

The funeral was in a nearby town. Tim was made aware of this through reading a newspaper article about the 'tragic death of missing boy's father'. He was taken by a neighbour as mum said she couldn't face it, there was a lot she couldn't face nowadays it seemed. She was distant and preoccupied most of the time, only occasionally remembering to take the time to check on how Tim was doing. Looking back Tim could now see that she was mostly in a chemically induced stupor, some psychopharmacology to help her through the long days. At the time it just felt like she was ignoring him.

It rained hard as they got out of the car, the kind of rain that soaks you if you so much as look at it. Everyone was forced to shelter under the entrance to the crematorium. It was then that he realised - he wasn't sure how he knew, but he did - that he was rubbing shoulders with the new family his dad had acquired. A woman in black holding an infant wrapped in a blanket and two small girls who looked overwhelmed. In spite of the fact they were related there was little that any of them could think to say to one another. Tim withstood the awkward silence for as long as he was able before asking the neighbour to take him home.

He returned to the house, not mentioning dad's new family to mum. They never spoke about them and Tim never tried to contact them, nor they him. Life continued in the same way it had done for some time now – mum was a ghost and he was a shadow.

With the payout from the insurance policy there was a sizable sum of money that now sat, mostly unused, in the building society. He drew some out on his next morning off and took it to the electrical outlet store where he sought advice on the best camera for filming in the dark, from a distance.

The shop assistant was both knowledgeable and helpful, bombarding Tim with an array of questions and some impressive-sounding technical jargon that Tim completely failed to understand. Having ascertained that the camera would be for filming wildlife in his back garden at night, the assistant produced a box that he assured Tim would be perfect for the job and asked if he wanted a demonstration. Having reached saturation point with specifications and descriptions Tim politely declined, paid and left.

Once he was at home he began to regret his decision. He sat drinking tea while the box sat on the table looking back at him, daring him to open it. He had already shouted up the stairs that he had the camera, clearly though, he was on his own with this. He continued to slurp his tea and thought to himself 'what would Ian do?'

The answer he came up with was only helpful in a roundabout way. He was certain that Ian would get the camera out and intuitively fiddle and fuss with it until, with no apparent effort, it was fully functioning. The logical answer seemed to be that he should do the opposite of that.

Opening the box, he carefully unpacked all the various components and spread them across the table, looking carefully at each item to determine what it was.

Next he opened the instruction booklet and read through the guide to getting started – twice. Once he was happy that he knew what he was supposed to do he set it up and put the battery on to charge. He was as confident as he could be that everything was good to go. There was one last thing to do, a test run. As he would have to wait until it was dark to do that he started to make himself some tea and switched the TV on while he waited for the sun to set.

Eventually his patience was rewarded. The charging light had turned green and the last of the day's sun had disappeared from the sky. He checked everything was working, put on his coat, put the instruction book in his pocket – just in case – then went out into the night.

He had already decided that the train station was the ideal place to test the camera; the size of the car park and the lighting conditions were similar to his workplace, it was close to home and he was likely to see people moving about as trains arrived and departed. He went straight there and sat himself down on a bench on the far side of the car park to the station building.

There were only a few cars in the car park, with it being late in the day. When he first arrived the area was deserted. He waited patiently, checking the camera controls once more before holding it on his lap and letting the shadows engulf him. He made a mental note to cover the bright red recording light with his finger as it glowed conspicuously in the dark.

Before too much time had passed the imminent arrival of a train was heralded by a young couple walking across the car park and into the station entrance. They were followed by a car dropping off a man with a suitcase. Tim filmed them as they went in, practising using the zoom and trying his best to keep them in the viewfinder. He waited for the train to arrive, then filmed the passengers who came out the station: a group of young lads in tracksuits, the male half of the couple that had arrived earlier and an older man who swayed visibly as he made his way across the car park.

Tim was still unsure if he'd had enough practise to ensure he would get it right if the two men turned up at the supermarket again on Monday night. He decided that it would be best, on balance, if he waited for the next train to give it one more go.

If he had been more familiar with the train timetable he might have thought better of this idea. The train that had just departed was due to run to the end of the line, wait for a short period and then return. It was about forty - five minutes before there was any new activity at the station; he filmed what there was. A car turned up and disgorged a pair of young women, the tracksuit lads from earlier returned to the station and a group of friends turned up in a noisy gaggle – fussing around saying goodbye and hugging and kissing until they split into two groups (train passengers and car passengers) and went their separate ways.

Tim decided he had probably taken enough footage now and returned home to sit back at the table and review the clips he had taken. After fumbling with the controls he eventually got the camera to play back. The man in the shop had said the picture would be grainy, and it was. But overall the features and details were clear enough to see, even on the tiny built in screen of the camera.

CHAPTER 13
Sergeant Crowley

Wendy was partnered with Mark again. She was unaware that he had requested this. He had told sergeant Crowley that he thought she had the potential to be a good officer and he didn't want her to be put off before she even started. Crowley was an old hand, due to retire at the end of the year. He didn't need Mark to explain what he meant; the gung-ho attitude of some of the younger lads and the way they behaved around the female officers, was a source of great irritation to him at times. Of course, nobody ever complained – they were always too scared of being ostracised by their peers. But he knew it went on, had seen it for himself. And he had seen Wendy's potential too, intelligent, but with street smarts, not learnt from a book. She read people well too, and could get along with people easily. He had already seen her comforting victims of crime in a way that he knew he never could.

Wendy was with Mark getting ready to leave the station, going through the routine of checking they had all their equipment, and that it was all working as it should. She found this both helpful and reassuring as she continued to feel her way into her role and learn the ropes.

"Can we do a drive-by at the supermarket later?"

"Sure, no problem, although I'd have thought you'd have seen enough of that place for today. What are we looking for?"

"I told Tim we would, he's worried that people have been stealing the trolleys."

She had nearly said 'the broken trolleys' but had stopped herself when she realised how improbable that sounded. Mark was about to answer, before he could he was interrupted by a laugh. Two other officers, 'Boyo' Boyce and 'Lanky Pete' had been standing close to them.

"Are you sure you don't just want to refer that straight to CID?" asked Lanky Pete.

"Or maybe counter terrorism?" added Boyo.

They both laughed again and Wendy felt herself blush. She looked towards Mark, who was about to reply to the two men – his cheeks had a hint of red to them and his brow was creased in the middle. But once again Mark was cut off before he could say his piece. Not Pete or Boyce this time, a quiet voice with a residual hint of a Brummie accent. Sergeant Crowley was neither big nor loud, he was about five foot eight with short grey hair, a matching beard and slight build – most of the other officers towered over him. He had built his reputation around his dedication to the job, his insistence and expectation that others would live up to the standards he kept for himself - and his track record.

"Excuse me?"

When Crowley said excuse me, you excused him; the laughter and conversation stopped abruptly and the group looked in his direction, but his green-eyed gaze was only on one person – Wendy. Her blush grew deeper as she made eye contact with him.

"Did you say it was Tim that asked you to look in on the supermarket?"

Wendy was momentarily flustered, if she had tried to guess what she was going to be asked that would not have been on her list.

"Er, yes. I don't know how sure he is, so far it's only the broken ones that are going missing. I'm sorry, I know it's silly but..."

She tailed off and braced herself, knowing that this would be the moment she found out why people were so deferential to the sergeant, she would be taken to one side and told not to waste time and resources on a whim and a rumour – or broken supermarket trolleys. Worse still, she may get reprimanded here, in front of everybody. Crowley spoke again.

"If we let one thing go, we might as well let everything go, and I'm not prepared to do that. I want the supermarket monitored every hour tonight, a loop of the car park and get out of the car and check the area by the loading bay. Boyce and Pete, that's your job tonight. I want it logged - and I will check."

He looked at Wendy, "Thank you for bringing it to our attention, have a good shift."

He went back to what he was doing, silently indicating that the conversation was now over. Lanky Pete and Boyo looked daggers at Wendy as Mark took her elbow and guided her out to the car. They sat in, before he started the engine he looked over to Wendy, "Tell me about the trolleys again."

"Just that Tim, who's kind of in charge of them, asked me to say that some had been going missing."

She thought then that he had looked as if he was on the verge of asking her something else, but he hadn't. Just the missing trolleys.

"Hmm, something perked Jim up though. It'll teach those other two a lesson."

"I hope they don't think I planned that."

"No, it's the sarge they'll grumble about. They'll keep quiet about it though, and hope he doesn't make them do it again tomorrow night too. C'mon then, criminals to catch. Let's get going."

"More like drunks to caution, but if you insist."

"If I didn't know better I'd think you were starting to sound cynical already," said Mark as he started the engine and they pulled out of their parking space and into the night.

Chapter 14
Stake Out

Tim didn't often wish his days away, he knew only too well how precious they were, and how wasteful that was. But on Monday he could hardly wait for his shift to end and the day to wind down. He went through the motions of his day, collecting trolleys and keeping the tarmac clear, until it was finally time to go home.

He ate his tea early, checked and then rechecked that the new camera was charged and ready to go then sat impatiently at the kitchen table.

"I'm going back again tonight," he called through the open kitchen door. "I'm going to see if those men come back, I'll be ready for them if they do."

The house was silent, apart from the small TV in the kitchen that he had switched on and then ignored.

"I'll probably be out all night again, if they come back I'll be there with this."

He held up the new camera, admiring it once more and wondering to himself why he had not thought of getting one before. He knew the answer though; what would he film? Family? Holidays? Parties? None of those things really featured in his day to day life, his was a solitary existence most of the time.

Eventually the clock ticked down the hours to what he had decided was the best time to leave. He picked up the things he had put out ready earlier, made one last check, then left for the supermarket.

As it had been previously, it was quiet. Lights were on deep inside the shop but the frontage was dark. Tim settled into his chair in the shadow of the wall and waited.

A car came into the car park and Tim sat up, alert with his camera at the ready. He watched as the driver and passenger got out, then slumped back again and watched as they changed places. The car hopped, stalled and spluttered its way slowly around the wide open space, he could see the passenger leaning across to adjust the steering. When it passed close to him he could see the teenage features of the driver, her face a mixture of excitement, fear and concentration. The passenger held a similar expression, without the excitement. Eventually the car came to an abrupt halt, they changed places and drove off into the night, the car now remembering how to behave itself.

Gradually the background noises quietened as the world went to sleep, lights of distant houses dimmed and noises of passing cars became less frequent. There was only one more visitor to the car park before midnight; a police patrol car pulled in, did a single circuit and then exited again. The officers in the car were two young men, not Wendy. Nevertheless Tim hoped that maybe the visit had been made in response to his request.

The night crept slowly along and Tim dozed, jerking upright whenever his head started to fall to one side. A fox sauntered across the open space, out on his evening rounds. Tim picked up the camera and started filming it almost without thinking, as it paused to sniff inquisitively at the air then made its way around the corner of the building. The camera was still in his hand when it reappeared ten minutes later; Tim started recording again.

This time the fox had lost its former insouciance, it had somehow contrived to get a small yellow bucket stuck on its head, it was walking backwards, trying to shake and scrape the offending item off. In spite of its obvious discomfort it made a comical sight as it backed around and scratched with his front paws trying to free his trapped ears. Tim did not leave it long before he switched the camera off and stood up, with the intention of attempting to rescue the creature.

As he got to his feet the bucket came loose and clattered onto the floor. The fox sniffed it once before turning and trying to reclaim its dignity as it strutted into the night. Tim returned to his vigil.

Following the same pattern as the previous Monday, Tim waited until the early hours of the morning. A thin mist had started to curl at the edges of the areas that were lit and the temperature dipped to its lowest point. By now he was sure that it was going to be another wasted night. He started to collect his things together, putting his flask in his backpack as he yawned and thought how good his bed was going to feel.

The BMW drove across to the same place it had parked the last time Tim had seen it. He sank back into his chair, switched the camera on and started to film as he heard the distinctive sound of a Land Rover approaching in the distance, the sound travelling through the still night air. The driver got out and looked around the car park, as his gaze turned towards him he realised that he had not covered the red light. Certain he had already been seen he quickly put his finger over it as the man's head turned in his direction and held his breath until the eyes peering through the dark had passed him and he was sure he had gone unnoticed. Finally the Land Rover came to a stop and the drivers greeted one another before going through the same routine as they had the previous week. Once he had zoomed shakily in on the exchange of the packet he waited until the cars had both left, switched off the camera then hurried home.

Chapter 15
Inertia

It was too late for Tim to go to bed now, and too early for him to do anything productive, he would sleep later. He placed the camera on the table, found the cables he needed to plug it into the TV and sat and watched back his footage, fast forwarding through his earlier experiments to get to the point of the BMW arriving.

It was, if he was honest, a little disappointing. It was still hard to make out the details of the men's faces and the number plates were not quite distinguishable. However, the overall quality of the image, in spite of the shakiness, the deep shadow and fuzzy quality, was enough to show clearly what was happening. Now he had to decide what to do with his newly acquired evidence, who to show it to and what to tell them. He toyed with the idea of showing it to Wendy, but didn't know if that would be sufficient. Maybe he should take it directly to the police station – he was undecided.

Over the years he had often found himself in this place of indecision, not able to commit to one course of action or another. As always when this happened, he deferred to what he imagined his brother would do. He asked the question out loud, "Wendy, or the police station?"

Then he sat looking at the frozen image on the TV screen while he considered the answer. He liked Wendy, he was sure it was her that had got the patrol cars to make night time visits to the car park, so she could clearly get things done. In his experience the police as a whole did not have a good track record when it came to getting things done - or finding people. He didn't know whether to trust them with this information or not, why would he? What would Ian do?

Of course, he did not always follow the imagined advice of his long-disappeared brother. There were times when he knew exactly what Ian would have done, but chose not to do it anyway. For instance, Ian would have continued to throw himself wholeheartedly into the social maelstrom of school, he would have gone to parties, had girlfriends, played on the soccer team, gone underage drinking, had fights and feuds and adventures. He would have done all of that with Tim, only he wasn't there – so neither of them did. School had been a lonely time, everybody else moved on and forgot about Ian, or pretended it didn't happen. But how could he do that when his brother's absence dominated his life? Also, since 'the incident' – as it came to be called – parents, locally and nationally, had been wary about letting their precious offspring out unchaperoned. Playparks were often deserted at first, then filled with parents who glanced at their watches and made small talk with each other while they waited to return to their usual activities. Evening clubs ended with huddles of teenagers in doorways, waited to be collected and escorted safely home. Even if Tim had wanted to meet up with friends, it would have been hard.

Ian would definitely have gone away to university if he had had the chance. Tim did not. For Tim the wrench of leaving the last place he had seen his twin would have been too much. Knowing that, if Ian came back or was found, this was the place it would happen. This is what anchored him here. The thought that he might be in the wrong place terrified him, in the past he had even found it hard to leave the house at times, scared that he would miss something.

The fear never left him, everywhere he went he constantly scanned the faces in the crowds – looking for someone who looked like him. Hopefully wishing that he would see someone who was as lost and alone as he was himself. Sometimes he even thought he did, a glimpse of someone wearing the same jumper that Ian had been wearing the last time he saw him, the same colour hair, a similar smile. It always stopped him in his tracks, then he had to stop himself from doubling back and checking, because he knew he was wrong even though he wished he was right.

His life hung on this wish, all his choices, every decision, each action was weighed up against the possibility that he might or might not be reunited with his brother.

He decided, in the way that young men do, that in a town with only one supermarket that was the place that Ian was most likely to wash up in the fullness of time. So he took the job in the car park when he left school and had spent his days since then scrutinising the features of the customers as they entered and left, hoping to see something – anything – that would give him hope.

The physicality of his work had helped him with the problems he had sleeping in the years after Ian vanished, lying awake wondering what happened, what was the last thing Ian did? Where did he go to? Who knew what happened? Somebody, somewhere, knew, and the thought kept Tim awake. When he did sleep he was frequently woken by terrible dreams where Ian was disposed of in every horrific and unimaginable way possible. Eventually his mum had noticed the dark circles under his eyes and his lethargic non-existence as he dragged his way through the endless days, dreading the coming night.

The therapist he was sent to could do little to convince him that he had things out of perspective or that he was exaggerating the problem. Mostly because he didn't and he wasn't. The medication she prescribed did help with the sleeping, but managed to intensify his zombie-like state during the day. Eventually he gave up both the sessions and the pills, but at times of stress the dreams and invasive thoughts returned confusing and diminishing him.

This was definitely a time of stress, what had started as a moment of intrigue and mystery had now led to the point where he needed to make a decision. He paced around the kitchen, vacillating about what he should do with his video. The problem had grown exponentially in his mind, leading to confusion and uncertainty.

Chapter 16
An Awful Shift

In her small, tidy flat a short distance from the centre of town, Wendy was also awake. Sitting at the kitchen table, wrapped in her dressing gown and nursing a mug of tea, she was deep in thought.

Last night had not gone well. Mark was not on shift, which wouldn't normally bother Wendy as she had worked alongside many of the other regulars before. But last night she had been partnered with Lanky Pete, who was evidently still smarting from Sergeant Crowley's rebuke. He grunted a greeting and they sat in silence as they set off on their evening rounds.

Lanky Pete drove directly to the supermarket, where he drove silently and with exaggerated slowness around the perimeter before returning to their proper route. The supermarket had still been open, with people coming in and out to their cars. As they drove away he asked Wendy, "See anything suspicious then?"

She sighed inwardly, it was going to be one of those nights.

"Only a squad car kerb crawling," she tried to joke.

"Don't want to stop and count the trolleys then?" he asked sarcastically.

She didn't answer, and Lanky Pete didn't offer any other conversational gambits until they got to the town centre where he asked her to 'have a word' with a group of teens who were hanging around harmlessly on some benches.

As Pete got slowly out of the car she went over and spoke to them, they were polite – if a bit cheeky – and assured her they were just 'hanging and chatting' and would be off home soon. Then Pete arrived, "Right you lot, we've had complaints about the mess and noise around here recently. Go on, off you go, the lot of you."

The kids grumbled and muttered under their breath as they reluctantly moved off, presumably to sit somewhere else out of sight of Wendy and Pete.

"That's how you deal with them," Pete told Wendy, "don't put up with their backchat."

"They weren't doing any harm, they were just kids hanging out with their friends."

"You've still got a lot to learn haven't you?" said Pete as he turned back to the car.

She did, but not from Pete. She knew that Mark would have spent some time talking to the group, found out their names and where they went to school in a conversational way. He would have set them up for the time when they needed to deal with the police, so they would be able to do so confident in the knowledge that someone would listen to them. Evidently that someone would not be Pete.

The evening continued in mostly awkward silence. Wendy was inwardly fuming, but didn't want her colleague to have the satisfaction of knowing he had riled her. She worked through the evening, doing what needed to be done. She made sure to remember what Mark had been patiently explaining to her, what she knew to be true, that they see people who are at their most vulnerable. People who need help and support. People who want to be made to feel safe. She also knew it was her duty to be assured and confident, to be the person who knew what she was doing even when she was unsure or even scared.

Pete kept niggling away at her, scoffing at her 'namby-pamby social worker approach' – as he so delicately put it. Undermining several of her decisions, puffing his chest out and using his height to let people know he was bigger (and better) than them.

As awful as the shift was, everything that happened in the early part of the evening paled into insignificance by the time the night was through.

It was full dark, things had started to quiet down, the pubs had closed and the last of the weeknight drinkers were on their way home in taxis, on buses or on foot. Thankfully it had passed without anything more than a noisy argument that had ended when Pete threatened to arrest both men, then a shop alarm that was ringing continuously. They had been asked to wait for the owner to arrive and shut it off so they could do a quick check of the premises with her. She had arrived promptly and, thankfully, it was nothing more than a glitch in the alarm system.

Wendy was watching the minutes count down to the end of this long and frustrating night when a call came over the radio of an RTA close to their location. Pete didn't respond, didn't even acknowledge the call.

"Aren't we going to answer that? It's near us," Wendy asked.

"It'll take us into overtime, the boss doesn't like that."

"But there's nobody else close."

"They can wait for a bit, it'll just be some stupid kid who's run his souped-up Fiesta into a wall."

"We should respond."

Pete let out a huge sigh, rolled his eyes and picked up the radio.

"Okay then, but if I'm late home I'm holding you personally responsible," he told Wendy as he let control know they were on their way to the scene.

This wasn't the first time Wendy had attended an accident. As Pete said, it was usually just someone who's had a minor shunt and things need to be calmed down, paperwork checked, breath tests administered and then everything logged for the various insurance companies involved. Tonight was not one of those.

As they turned into the street they were greeted with a scene that it took Wendy several moments to make sense of as they approached.

A red hatchback was propped on its side. The driver's door, now facing the sky, was crunched up like an empty crisp packet. Several people were around the car moving frantically as if looking for a way in. As Wendy and Pete arrived they stopped and looked expectantly towards them.

Further down the road, past the junction, was a second car. A blue Audi that was crumpled from the radiator grill to the windscreen, its wheels splayed outwards and steam rising from the now corrugated bonnet. The driver's door was open and a man in a dressing gown was bending to talk to whoever was crouched on the ground, leaning against the side of the car.

Between the two cars, lying on the road was a prone figure. More people were gathered: one woman with a blanket, another man on his phone and two more standing over the still lump.

The iridescent blue lights of their car flashed over the scene, creating an eerie glow and intermittently highlighting the details of the accident. Now everybody was looking at them, relief visible on their faces; 'the police are here', 'they'll know what to do'; 'thank goodness, help has arrived.'

"I'll radio in for support," Pete told her, "you take a quick look around."

Wendy didn't question him, she got out, putting on her Hi-Viz while trotting towards the first car. She looked around as the observers tried to give her their various accounts of what had happened and what the situation was;

"There's someone trapped in there."

"That woman's hurt."

"He was driving like a nutter."

"She just stepped right out in front of him, he had to swerve."

"Shall I get my first aid kit from the house?"

Bombarded with information, Wendy was finding it hard to think what she should do first. She blocked out the background noise, took a deep breath then stepped up to the upended car. Through the cracked windscreen she could see there was indeed someone trapped inside, dangling from his seatbelt with blood on his face and flaps of now deflated airbags folded around him. Looking at the windscreen she saw a corner of the glass was loose, she put her fingers underneath and pulled as hard as she could.

She was surprised when it actually came away, peeling back from the rubber seal. It came back far enough for her to put her face to the opening and speak to the driver.

"It's okay sir, help is on the way. Where are you hurt?"

"I've bashed me fucking head and me fucking leg's stuck. Get me the fuck out of here."

"Okay, the fire brigade are coming, is there anybody else in the car with you?"

"No, can you get them to fucking hurry up?"

"They're coming as fast as they can, stay calm and we'll have you out as quickly as possible."

Satisfied that someone who was able to swear at her with so much gusto wasn't about to pass away immediately, she asked one of the bystanders to keep talking to him through the gap, and let her know if he took a turn for the worse – not that she'd know what to do if he did. She then strode briskly, not quite running, to the person on the ground.

A woman in pink joggers and a blue sweatshirt, with a pair of still unlaced trainers on her bare feet was kneeling next to the inert form. She watched Wendy approach. As soon as she got close enough the woman spoke rapidly.

"I'm a nurse, this patient is unconscious and badly hurt, you'll need to get the first paramedics here straight away. I'll stay with her if you want to go and check the other car."

Thank goodness, Wendy thought, she wasn't on her own. Except she shouldn't be on her own. Where the fuck was Pete? She looked back to see him still by the car, the door was open and he was just gathering his Hi-Viz. What the fuck had he been doing?

She got to the second car and was nearly overwhelmed by the smell of fuel, so strong it made her eyes water. Her first thought was to move people away from the car, she approached the seated figures.

"We need to move away from the car - now."

She reached under the arm of the woman who had evidently been driving and, together with the dressing gown man, helped her to her feet and started to walk towards the pavement. The woman appeared dazed and confused but was compliant, moving uncertainly with the support of her human crutches. Wendy looked back at the steaming car, wondering if they were far enough away yet to be safe. As she turned her head the woman became agitated and began to pull away from her.

"My baby, my baby's in there."

She understood straight away, no chance to question why someone would have a baby in a car at this time of night, most likely just taking a night time drive to settle it.

"Stay here," she ordered, then ran back towards the car. As she got near she saw the first flicker of a flame from under the concertinaed front end. She wrenched the back door open and leant in. There on the back seat, fast asleep and smiling softly to itself all snuggled up in a furry blanket, was a baby. She snatched and fumbled at the safety harness, but it didn't fully open. She yanked at it in her frustration, then made herself stop and look more carefully. It was obvious now, she pressed the button that released the strap between the infant's legs and lifted it out. Clutching it to her chest she could smell the talcum powder and soap from its bath time. This lasted for the briefest of moments, before it was overwhelmed by the distinctive odour of burning, now strong in her nostrils. Turning, she ran towards the mother, who was being held back by dressing gown man. He also appeared to be mostly what was keeping her upright, a look of blind panic on her stricken face as she tried to struggle forward.

As Wendy took her first few steps, she heard a dull whump behind her. Instinctively she held the baby closer, sheltering it with her body, and ran faster as the flickering light of the flames from the now-burning car made her shadow stretch out in front of her, racing towards the mothers outstretched arms at the side of the road, and safety.

She handed the baby to the mother, tears streaming down her face. She snatched it eagerly and immediately began to inspect it, pulling it to her, kissing it, crying and telling it it was okay now over and over. The fuss woke the baby who now started to cry too, but the sound was lost to Wendy as she turned back to the scene, ordering people to move back and to leave space for the other emergency vehicles when they arrived.

Pete arrived at her side.

"Okay, I've got it now. Go and make sure that baby's okay."

Wendy stopped dead in her tracks and looked at the newly arrived Pete. The only thing that prevented her from giving him a fusillade of abuse was the near spontaneous arrival of the fire engine and ambulance, along with a second squad car.

Ignoring Pete, she began barking orders to the arriving teams. The firefighters immediately started work on dousing the flames from the burning car. Wendy spoke to the leading officer and told him about the man trapped in the side-up car, then hurried to the ambulance crew as they decamped with all their equipment, directing them to the stricken woman first, walking alongside them to let them know who else needed attention. They thanked her as they knelt down and started to receive a detailed handover from the nurse.

Now she looked around to see Sergeant Crowley striding towards them. He must have been in the other police car. His eyes scanned the scene taking it all in as he walked, then he stopped in front of Pete and asked abruptly, "Update?"

Pete floundered, looking towards Wendy as he started to tell Crowley that they were still assessing the scene and that it was all a bit of a mess. He started to describe what he thought might have happened to cause the accident. Wendy couldn't bear it and interrupted, "Sarge, male occupant in overturned car injured but lucid. Female pedestrian badly hurt, she has a nurse and the paramedics with her now. Second car had a female and an infant on board, neither seem badly hurt on initial observations – I'll direct the next ambulance crew there to take them in and check them over, especially the baby. No other casualties known at this time."

"Thanks, I'll pick that up if you and Pete want to seal off the area with tape and start getting the details of some of these witnesses, have a chat with them and check there's nothing we've missed."

With that he started to walk towards a newly arrived ambulance, directing the crew towards the wrecked car, which the fire crew were now busy disassembling. Pete started back to the car, to pick up the tape presumably. Wendy went in the opposite direction, back to the mother and baby who were now sitting on a chair which had been procured from someone's house.

She knelt beside them and asked the baby's name. The mother, now calmer, told her it was Ezra.

"Well, you and Ezra are safe now," this seemed to be true, the fire had been extinguished with a sea of foam and sand was being scattered around the spilt fuel on the ground. "I'm going to stay with you for a moment until the ambulance crew can get to you. They'll take you into Central and check you and Ezra over. Is there anyone you need to get in touch with?"

"My husband, somebody already called him."

On cue a car stopped a hundred yards down the road and a man in shorts and a hoodie leapt out. Leaving the door open and the engine running he ran as fast as he could towards them, looking in panic at the burnt out car and the scene of devastation. Wendy intercepted him, "It's okay sir, slow down everybody's okay. You must be Ezra's dad right?"

"Yes, where are they?"

"Over here," Wendy led him to them then stepped back as the family reunited and talked over one another in rushed and panicked tones. She went to the abandoned car and carefully parked it at the side of the road before taking the keys to the owner. As she passed them to him he looked at her, "You're the one who saved them?"

"No, I just moved them to a safe place."

"That's not what everyone else is saying, you got Ezra out of the car when it was on fire."

He took her hand and shook it, and she didn't really know what to say or do. The burst of adrenaline that had carried her so far had peaked and was now subsiding, and yes, maybe she did get a baby out of a burning car. But that was all just part of the job, wasn't it?

"I'm just glad that everyone's okay, sir, go and be with your family. He's a beautiful baby by the way, I can't believe he slept through most of this."

She smiled and the father smiled back, "Thank you so much, really."

"It was nothing, go on, they need you."

Feeling a wave of exhaustion hit her she moved herself away from the busy scene, everything seemed to be in hand now, she rested briefly against a low wall. More ambulances and a second fire crew had turned up, along with what seemed like all of the oncoming shift from the police station. As she looked around she saw Sergeant Crowley striding towards her, she hurriedly got to her feet.

"Sorry, sarge, just taking a moment."

"You take as many moments as you want," he answered. "It'll take some time to finish up here, but from what I've heard you did well."

"Thank you sir, it was only…" what? She didn't know what it was only, just that when it mattered she was able to step up. But now her mind was running over and over what had happened, had she done it right? Could she have done more? She felt a hand on her elbow and looked up to see that it was Crowley, guiding her towards an ambulance.

"This is your ride, you need to go and get checked out."

"But I'm fine, sarge."

"What I've heard is that you were in a burning car this evening, you're getting a once over at the hospital – and that's an order."

"I think that may be an exaggeration, I was only…"

"Stop arguing and get in the back, I'll send someone to wait with you and they'll drive you home afterwards."

At this point a paramedic arrived and steered Wendy into the ambulance, placing a blanket on her shoulders and starting to fire questions at her. Crowley retreated, the doors shut and the ambulance moved off.

Now, alone in her flat, she has been given a clean bill of health. She has already made several pages of notes about what happened, before her memory becomes hazy or confused, ready to go into her full report. She has an overwhelming desire to sleep, but her mind is racing, replaying, questioning and – if she is being honest with herself – having a delayed panic attack.

Chapter 17
A Quiet Night In

Tim decided, he would ask Wendy what she thought he should do, see what she made of the nocturnal goings on in the car park. But he didn't see Wendy the next day, he kept a look out for her and even went inside a couple of times to see if he had missed her and she was on a checkout. He kept busy while he waited, between the bus from town and the senior citizens celebrating pension day, there was plenty to do.

He found Sonia from the café when she took her break, to ask if she had seen Wendy. His question has to wait though, as Sonia immediately holds out her left hand in front of Tim. At first he's not sure what he's meant to be looking at, then the penny drops and he expresses his admiration for the band of gold with its small sparkling stone. Sonia starts to tell him excitedly about the plans she has for their wedding, of course it won't be for a while as they need to save some money for the event.

Tim listens attentively as Sonia describes the dress she is planning to wear and the people she wants to invite, "Of course you'll have to come Tim, I insist. Anyway, listen to me going on, how are you?"

He told her he was fine – which is not untrue, he was just a bit tired. Then he slipped in his question about Wendy. The broad smile on Sonia's face manages to stretch even wider, if that's possible.

"She was on the rota today, but she hasn't shown up. I can ask if anyone knows why if you want, I thought I saw you two talking the other day."

Sonia doesn't miss much when it comes to gossip, she likes to know what's going on and is well placed to find out in her little café nook. She winked at Tim and waited expectantly for him to spill the beans. This flustered him slightly, he felt himself blush and took his eyes away from Sonia's.

"No, it's nothing like that, it's a, uhm, well, it's kind of a work thing."

"Okay, sorry, I didn't mean to embarrass you, I was just teasing. If I hear anything I'll let you know okay, now you have a good afternoon."

"Okay, thanks, Sonia, and congratulations again."

They went their separate ways. Tim decided he might not ask anyone else if they had seen Wendy, he didn't really want her shifts to be plagued with everyone's speculation. Although it hadn't been on his mind when he approached her, he had to admit to himself that he found her attractive. Maybe subconsciously that was why he had chosen to talk to her first. She was roughly his age, but unlike his local peers she was from out of town, so probably didn't know his history.

Previous romantic encounters had all been tinged with curiosity: the novelty factor of a macabre local celebrity. At least, that was how it had felt to him, and feeling like that had made it hard for him to go out with girls. He was always waiting for the inevitable questions about Ian; it always felt to him that it was his brother girls were really interested in. These awkward conversations that would lead to him becoming withdrawn and ending the relationship.

The day carried on. Every time he passed the area of the car park where the exchange had taken place he slowed, pausing to look as if there might be some unnoticed clue, or as though the tarmac itself might hold the answers to his questions. He fought off his fatigue until it was time for him to finish, no hanging around for him tonight. He collected a ready meal from inside and went directly home.

"I'm home, I didn't see Wendy today. I still don't really know what I should do."

He put the meal in the microwave; small bleeps sounded as he entered the required instructions.

"I think I'll wait and see if she's in tomorrow, I don't really want to go to the police station. They'll just laugh at me, like that time I thought I'd seen you on the TV."

He remembered the day vividly, the person on duty on the desk hadn't understood what Tim had been telling him to start with. When he finally did get it, he told Tim in a condescending tone that they didn't have the time or manpower to sit and scan the entire crowd at the cup final just to see if they could spot Ian. He told him it really was most unlikely, but that he should keep an eye out anyway and only come back if he had something definite for them to go on. Tim was embarrassed, certain that the man was mocking him, and turned to leave. But before he could leave the building another policeman, a sergeant, had stopped him. He recognised his face, he was one of the people who had been omnipresent at his house when Ian had first vanished. He remembered the officer had been kind to him then, and he was kind again now. He took Tim quietly to one side and told him, promised him, that he would get a tape of the match and look. He was sincere, assuring Tim that nobody had forgotten his brother and that they were still looking, although it was getting harder the more time passed.

"Yeah, that's what I'll do, see if she's there tomorrow. I'm having a fish pie for tea, guess that's just me then."

Of course it was just him, Ian had always hated fish. Tim laughed to himself as he remembered how Ian had used to hold his nose between his thumb and forefinger and make gagging noises on the rare occasions mum had tried to make any fish based meals. Although fish fingers were completely acceptable for some reason, especially when they were wrapped in white bread with a generous amount of ketchup.

"Anyway, I'm knackered. I'm going to bed once I've eaten this."

He didn't though; after he had finished he watched his video again. He ran through the four minute clip several times, hoping to see some detail he had missed, before he finally gave up for the evening, showered then slept.

Chapter 18
Debrief

The words appear painfully slowly on the screen, frequently disappearing again to be replaced by slightly different words with roughly the same meaning. Writing had never been Wendy's favourite activity, she was more of a numbers person. Her handwritten notes helped fill the gaps in her memory, although most of the events were still clear in her mind – way too clear.

The accident had invaded her dreams last night, exaggerating the events, providing different and more horrific outcomes and getting confused with the storylines of several different films. In the cold light of day she now realised that she had been either reckless and foolhardy or unthinkingly brave, probably a mixture of the two she thought.

She had been trying to describe the events in clear, concise and non-emotive language. It was hard as she couldn't help recalling how she had felt and the way people had been reacting to the unfolding events. She was also struggling to describe Lanky Pete's involvement – or lack of - in her report. After the events of earlier in the evening, combined with his initial reluctance to even attend the accident, she was not feeling well disposed towards him. Eventually she decided that Pete could write about his own contribution himself, it wasn't her problem.

The hustle and bustle of the busy office behind her had largely receded into the background as everybody went about their business. Phone calls, conversations, meetings and greetings were all just white noise while she concentrated on getting the details of the incident right. She actually jumped when a hand landed on her shoulder, whirling around to see Sergeant Crowley's smiling face.

"I'm sorry," he said, "I didn't mean to startle you."

"It's okay, I was in a world of my own."

"Well sorry anyway, can I have a quick word with you?"

"Sure," Wendy leant back in her chair expecting Crowley to pull up another chair or perch on the edge of the desk.

"Not here, let's find somewhere quieter." He led the way to a side office and Wendy locked her computer screen, got up and apprehensively followed him.

"Here, this is better. Close the door up would you, please."

He seemed friendly, but previous experiences of being taken into offices for 'a chat' had never been positive for Wendy. She closed the door and sat in the chair opposite Crowley.

"You look terrified, it's okay, I just wanted to check in with you."

Wendy relaxed a little, glad not to be in trouble.

"I just wanted to check in on you, make sure you're okay after last night."

"Oh, I'm fine. They gave me a thorough going over at the hospital, all fine."

"That's good, but actually I already knew that. It was the other sort of okay I wanted to ask about. An event like that can be very traumatic."

"Oh, no I'm fine. I mean I didn't sleep that well, but I think I'm alright. I changed my work shifts so I could get some rest today."

" Good thinking, it won't be for much longer, I'm looking forward to having you on the team full time. I have to say, I know there can be a very macho attitude around the station sometimes, not always a healthy one. I went home and cried after my first RTA, and I suspect most of the other guys did too, although you'd never get many of them to admit it. We've got counselling you can access if you feel it would help."

"Actually, just knowing it's not only me that feels like this is a huge help."

This was true, Wendy had thought she would be expected to shrug it off and move on, all part of the job. She was relieved to know that at least one person could empathise with how she was feeling.

"Anyway, well done you. I heard some stories from the witnesses at the scene last night, seems you were quite the hero."

"There may have been some exaggeration there, I didn't really do much at all."

"Don't ever tell yourself that, Wendy, there are people alive today who may not have been if it wasn't for your unselfish decisiveness and prompt actions. It made me proud to hear people talking about someone on my watch the way they were talking about you."

Wendy was full on blushing now, she didn't know what to say, so she settled for muttering her thanks. Crawley wasn't finished.

"It's not unusual for people to freeze at moments like that, not be sure what to do first. It's natural, and much more common than you would think. You shouldn't judge when that happens, it will have been a learning experience for them. I'm pretty sure you understand what I'm saying."

Wendy was pretty sure she did. She had thought about what had happened and how it could have been better. For some of this time she had been silently cursing Lanky Pete for his lack of support when they arrived. Now, thanks to the sergeant, she saw this for what it was; a brief paralysis. So he hadn't run over with her, but he had made sure that the back-up they needed was all en-route and made sure control had the necessary information to get the right support to them.

"Yes, sarge, everything's good. I'm just glad everyone was okay."

She had already checked of course. The man had been lifted from the upturned car and had mostly superficial injuries; the pedestrian had head and leg injuries but was conscious, plastered up and not in a serious condition. Baby Ezra and his mum had been kept overnight for observation but appeared to have suffered no adverse consequences from the accident.

"Good, I've got a quieter night for you tonight. I want you to stay here and sort through some paperwork I've got backlogged, I'll pop it on your desk in a minute. Then go home early and get a proper night's sleep, okay?"

She thought she would be disappointed at being kept back, but actually found she was relieved knowing she wouldn't be called on for any more stressful life and death situations for one evening. She gave a silent thank you to Crowley before taking herself back to the computer she had been working at.

Chapter 19
The Tape

Tim finally caught up with Wendy, the following afternoon.

She came out to the car park during her break to look for him.

"Hi, Tim, Sonia said you'd been looking for me, is everything okay?"

Although Tim was glad to see her, he kind of wished he hadn't said anything to Sonia. The last thing he wanted was for Wendy to be talked about by the other staff. Still, too late now, what's done is done.

"Yes, it's all fine. It's kind of silly really, I wanted to ask you something."

"Well fire away. Is it to do with the trolleys?"

"No, well kind of yes but not really. It's sort of difficult to explain."

"Try me."

"It's complicated, maybe it would be easier to show you. Would you be able to come to my house this evening?"

Wendy was intrigued; if this was an elaborate pick up line it had got her interest. If it was really just about the trolleys that was okay too, it would be nice to have a chance to talk to Tim somewhere apart from the car park. She had no reason to believe that he was an axe murderer or people trafficker and she actually had an evening off for a change, so why not?

"Sure, what time?"

"Ah, oh, maybe around eight. If you're sure you don't mind."

She assured him she didn't mind and he gave her his address before they went about their respective businesses. Tim arranged to get away quickly, getting one of the guys from the loading bay to take over from him. Nobody minded, he had covered for all of them at one time or another and got on with them in his quiet and unobtrusive way.

Arriving home he looked around the house, trying to imagine what a visitor would see. A large pile of books next to an overstuffed bookcase, some faded décor, a few old family photos in frames and a clean tidy kitchen. It seemed mostly alright, but nevertheless he ran the hoover round, dusted some surfaces, sprayed air freshener about and transported some of the book mountain upstairs to the back bedroom where they got dumped unceremoniously on the bed.

"I'm just putting these here for now. I've got someone coming round and I don't want the house to look a mess. I'll tidy them up later; maybe even get rid of a few."

He surveyed the heap of books, most of which he had read and decided that a trip to the charity shop was needed sometime soon. He went back downstairs to check the kitchen, ensuring he had supplies of tea, coffee, milk and biscuits. There was enough, even though he rarely, if ever, had visitors. In fact, he couldn't remember the last time anybody had called around. He kept himself to himself and that seemed to suit other people as much as it suited him. He changed out of his work clothes, showered and put on his jeans and a baggy checked shirt. After pulling his hair into a ponytail he checked the camera was all set up, then waited for Wendy to arrive.

Wendy had gone through a similar showering and changing routine, dithering over her selection of non-work clothes. She didn't want to turn up in her scruffiest outfit, but also didn't think full-on going out clothes were right either. She settled for a pair of jeans and a comfortable blue and red shirt, warm enough for the walk over to Tim's house. Unsure whether to go empty handed or not she took a bottle of wine from the kitchen counter with her. It had sat there for longer than she could remember. She had purchased it on a whim but been unwilling to open it for a single glass, knowing that most of it would end up turning to vinegar in the fridge.

The doorbell rang at precisely eight. Even though he had been expecting it, the unfamiliar noise made Tim start slightly; he took one more quick look around, then opened the door. Wendy started to speak, "Hi, I hope.."

She looked Tim up and down, then looked down at herself, "Oh, I see you got the memo." She laughed out loud and Tim was momentarily confused, then he realised what she had seen. They were wearing similar – almost to the point of identical - outfits. He laughed along as he stepped back from the door, although inside he was mortified.

"I can pop up and change if you want," he said.

"No, don't worry, it's fine really. We can be twins."

There was a brief moment of awkward silence, Tim stood frozen in the doorway and the seconds dragged out a fraction too long to be comfortable.

"I brought this, I don't know if you drink wine." She held out the bottle which broke Tim's awkward silence. He took it, thanking her profusely and ushering her into the kitchen where he offered to open it.

"Actually, if I'm honest I'd rather have a cup of tea if that's okay."

"That's fine, I'll get the kettle on, have a seat."

Wendy sat at the table while Tim organised mugs, milk and teabags. Looking around she saw a tidy, well-kept kitchen, healthy pot plants on the window ledge, clean surface, everything organised and in its place.

"You run a tight ship," she said.

"Thanks, I like to keep on top of things, it makes life easier."

What Tim did not say was that he had been doing this from a young age. When his dad had left and mum had withdrawn into herself it had been up to him to keep the house from descending into unordered chaos.

"I'm glad you can't see my kitchen right now, it's a mess."

"I'm sure it's not, anyway I'd have to take part of the blame for making you come here straight after work."

He put her tea on the table in front of her and sat down opposite with his own. She put it to her lips and sipped at the still steaming drink, smiling.

"It's not a problem, it's actually quite nice to be somewhere that's not home, work or the police station for a change. What was it you wanted to ask me anyway?"

"Well, you remember what I told you about the trolleys going missing?"

Wendy nodded and Tim then proceeded to tell her what had happened after he had decided to look into the matter himself. Wendy listened attentively without interrupting, she noticed a passing reference to a joint decision that Tim had made with Ian. She was going to ask who Ian was but didn't want to break the thread of the story, which was fascinating. She thought he had come to an end, when he told her about the mysterious liaison in the car park.

"My, you're right, that does sound suspicious. Did you get any closer or see what it was they were passing?"

Tim carried on, explaining about the camera and his return visit to the car park. Again, he referenced Ian in his decision making. Now Wendy was only interested in one part of the story though.

"So you filmed it happening?"

"Yes, that's why I wanted to talk to you. I can show it to you, you could have a look and see if it's anything important."

"I'd love to, have you got it here?"

"It's all set up and ready in the sitting room. I've plugged it into the tv."

They stood simultaneously and Wendy followed him into the adjoining room, taking a seat while Tim switched everything on and pressed play on the camera. It flickered into life as he sat down and started showing a short clip of the empty kitchen. The camera panned around and zoomed in and out randomly.

"Oh bollocks, I went back right to the start when I was setting the camera up. Sorry, I'll just fast forward it."

"Don't worry, I'm not in a rush."

"If you're sure, it won't be too long."

"It's fine," Wendy reassured him. They settled back and watched as Tim's kitchen turned into the station car park with people emerging from the doorway, then another flicker and another group of people started to walk back towards the station, again with some zooming and jerky panning of the camera.

"I just wanted to check it worked in the dark," Tim explained.

"Sensible, I would have done the same."

Now the scene changed again, Wendy watched the fox strolling majestically across the car park, "Isn't he beautiful? I sometimes see him when I'm on late shifts."

The fox returned, looking more ridiculous than majestic, they both laughed at its comical appearance.

"It's coming up next," Tim said.

They both sat forward in silence and watched attentively as headlights washed across the car park, came to halt and waited to be joined by the second car. Wendy was fully immersed now, straining to see every detail of the handover.

"Can we rewind it and watch it again?"

"Sure."

"This happens every Monday?"

"Definitely the last two Mondays, yes."

"Rewind it again."

Tim did, and they watched it a third time. When it had finished Wendy sat back and let out a long breath that she hadn't realised she was holding.

"They're up to something aren't they?"

She didn't say, but she thought that maybe this was a step towards finding out how the new influx of drugs were arriving in town. Although it was a small package, maybe they were doing it little and often rather than in bulk.

"Can I borrow the tape?"

"I can make a copy of it, but I'd rather you didn't say where you got it if you're taking it to the police station."

"No problem, any reason? Or is it none of my business?"

"I just don't want people to think I'm weird, spending my nights filming in the car park just because we lost some trolleys. People already think I'm a creep."

"I'm sure they don't."

Wendy meant this, spending a bit of time with Tim had been kind of soothing. He was gentle and quiet and had made her feel comfortable.

"They do, but I'm not, I just like to keep myself to myself. And the trolley thing got under my skin, nobody else seemed bothered about it. Well, until you did something."

"I get that, it's irritating when you know something's wrong and can't do anything about it. I'd like to show the tape to my colleagues and see what they make of it, no need to mention you at all."

"Okay, thanks."

His mind was more at rest now, and he had enjoyed having a visitor for the first time in forever. Also, he thought he was maybe starting to like Wendy now he was getting to know her a bit more. She didn't act like other people did around him sometimes, giving him a wide berth, talking down to him or dredging up old memories.

"Do you want me to open that wine?"

Wendy hadn't really anticipated drinking the wine, but now she had someone to share it with and she wasn't in a rush, it made sense.

"Go on then, let's live dangerously."

By the time the bottle was empty they were both fairly tipsy. She had shared what felt like most of her life story with Tim, who listened attentively and made appropriate disapproving noises when she described some of her previous friendships.

In turn he had volunteered information about his hobbies and interests – mostly reading and listening to music. They discovered that they had several mutual favourite bands in common, leading to Tim putting on a CD as they were talking. Wendy admitted to not having read a lot of books that she had always felt she should have, even though she enjoyed reading. She worried that she didn't really know where to start. They both agreed that there was nothing better than reading a Terry Pratchett book in bed at the end of the day.

Finally time got the better of them, Tim found a blank tape and copied the short burst of grainy film onto it.

"I'll talk to someone tomorrow, ask someone else to have a look, if that's okay?"

"That's fine, thank you."

"It's no trouble."

"No, I mean thank you for coming over, and thank you for not laughing at me."

"Don't be daft, I've had a nice evening, we should do it again sometime."

Tim leant against the door after it had closed and let out a long sigh. This was the most sociable he had been for a long time and he should have been exhausted from the effort of it. But he wasn't; it had been easy to talk to Wendy and he hoped she had been serious when she suggested they meet again.

Wendy walked home with the tape in her hand, a spring in her step and a smile on her face. She had only been on a couple of dates since Rob walked out on her. Neither of them had gone well, with both men seeming eager to get past the getting to know you formalities and into her bed. This had been different; it had been nice.

Chapter 20
Handover

She hesitated as her thumb hovered over the send button. She knew Mark was at work, and probably busy, but she didn't know who else to ask. She paused, then sent the message, *'Can I have a chat with you?'*

She was half way to putting her phone down on the kitchen counter when it rang, with Mark's name on the screen. He had given her his number in case she ever needed to ask him anything work related or needed a hand with anything.

"Mark, sorry to call you at work, I just wanted to ask you something."

"No need to apologise, I'm just catching up with things before I go out on patrol, I was going to call you anyway actually."

"Oh, okay," Wendy was puzzled for a moment ,until Mark continued.

"I just heard about the other night, are you okay?"

"The other night?"

"The night you ran into a blazing inferno to rescue a baby, that night."

"Oh that, yes I'm fine. I think you'll find people have been over-egging it slightly."

"There's no need to be modest, own it – just don't milk it."

"I get it, anyway I'm fine, the sergeant had a chat with me afterwards."

"I hope he had a chat with Lanky Pete too; from the sound of it he left you high and dry."

"It wasn't really like that, he just wasn't in the same position as me."

"Okay, I won't ask. Your trouble is you're too polite."

"Not really, but thanks for saying it anyway."

"So, what did you want?"

"Oh, that, yes. Well it's probably nothing, but I wanted to ask you about something."

"Like?"

"I've got a video of something that looks quite suspicious, I wondered if you would have a look at it before I take it to Crowley. I don't want to end up looking a plonker again."

"I doubt it, you're his golden girl right now. But sure, can you come in today?"

"Yes, but not until later."

"What time?"

"4ish."

"Perfect, I'll see you here and I'll have a coffee ready."

"Okay, thank you so much, I really appreciate it."

"There you go again with the polite…later."

He hung up, leaving Wendy surprised at how quickly he'd agreed to look at the tape, even without knowing what it was.

Her afternoon shift finished at three, which gave her just enough time to go home, change out of her garishly coloured work fleece and get to the station with the tape. Mark was waiting in the entrance, with two coffees.

"You didn't think I meant coffee from the canteen did you?" he laughed as he passed one to Wendy, fobbed them into the main body of the building and led through to one of the side rooms.

There was a TV already set up in the room, Wendy handed the tape to him and he put it on and pressed play. They then sat and watched the nocturnal car park transaction together. When it finished Mark stopped it and turned to her.

"Where is this?"

"The supermarket car park."

"When?"

Wendy gave him all the details she had, apart from who had given her the tape. He seemed satisfied when she told him her source had asked her not to say.

"Okay, wait here a moment."

He returned a few minutes later with Crowley.

"Hi, Wendy, how are you feeling?"

"Fine now, thanks."

"Good, Mark tells me you're making a bid to be the next chief constable," he smiled, "let's have a look at what you've got."

They watched the tape together, then Wendy answered near identical questions to the ones that Mark had asked her.

"I'm glad you bought this in, Wendy, is it okay if I keep it, I'm going to need to share it with upstairs. They may need to ask you some more questions, but I think they'll probably have enough for now. Do you mind waiting for a bit?"

"Not at all," she replied. Crowley took the tape and left the room. Mark leaned backwards and took a large gulp of his coffee.

"There you are again, being polite."

She smiled back at him and they talked while they waited for Crowley's return, Mark seemed to want every detail of the accident from the other night and interrupted her several times to tell her she'd made a good call or ask a question.

Crowley eventually returned.

"Thanks for waiting, I've left the tape with the Super. He was very interested in it, I think they're arranging a meeting to talk about it right now. There's no need for you to wait around, someone will be in touch if they need to know more. I'll see you on your usual shift. Sure you can't tell us how you came by it?"

"They were positive they didn't want me to say," she shrugged, "thanks, Sarge, see you tomorrow."

She said her goodbyes and walked out into the busy street, satisfied that she had done the right thing and keen to let Tim know how it went. She was actually quite looking forward to seeing him again, she'd had a nice evening yesterday. She didn't want to get her hopes up too much, but it might be fun getting to know him a bit better.

Chapter 21
Chocolates

The days passed quickly, Wendy saw Tim at work the following day to let him know that his tape had been handed on up to the detectives, who were very interested in it. This pleased Tim, which in turn made her happy to have been able to do something useful.

She suggested meeting up for a drink sometime, which he agreed to immediately, although they had not yet managed to agree a mutually convenient day, time or place. She had hoped he would get back to her, but had not heard from him yet, so she was waiting to catch him at work and give him some options. She isn't used to doing the chasing, so to speak, so doesn't want to appear too pushy – or desperate. Which is fair enough as she is neither of those things.

She also told him that it would probably be best to stay out of the car park at night for the time being, at least until the situation with the mystery cars had been looked into. He had agreed with her that that was probably a good idea. She had seen from the rota that extra staff had been drafted for the following Monday night and guessed that the information Tim had given her was about to be acted on, although she clearly could not let him know this.

For now Wendy immersed herself in her studies and kept up her exercise regime in preparation for her imminent career change from supermarket worker to full-time police officer.

Tim had also found the days were flying by, he had several long shifts and had been busy sorting out the books that he had relocated when Wendy visited. This had involved a thorough reorganising of his entire book collection, deciding on which were keepers, which could be donated, which still needed to be read and which would never be read.

Four bin bags full of books had been taken to local charity shops one bag at a time. He knew that they needed new homes, where they would be read, kept on shelves, shared and loved – rather than buried in a waist high pile on the floor. But it was still quite hard to part with them. The only books that were exempt from this cull were the ones on the bedroom bookcase. This selection of Goosebumps, Roald Dahl, Dr Seuss, Enid Blyton and other childhood favourites had been his and Ian's collection. They had both enjoyed reading and, unlike some of their other belongings, books were acknowledged to be communal possessions. Tim didn't read them, but every so often he would take one from the shelf, hold it in his hand and open it at a random page. Looking at the words on the page he would feel a connection to Ian, knowing that he was touching something that nobody apart from Ian and himself had ever used. It helped him when he was feeling lost.

The book sorting had unearthed some half-read books that Tim wanted to finish, and several new acquisitions that he needed to make the time for. Naturally this led to a reading binge that consumed a vast quantity of his spare time as he raced through a selection of literature that took him to different star systems, make-believe kingdoms and long-ago times.

As much as he enjoyed it, he knew that the reading binge was a displacement activity. He wasn't certain that Wendy's suggestion of going for a drink was an actual invitation or if she was just being polite. Even though he didn't really drink much or often, he had enjoyed spending the evening with her the previous week and very much wanted to see her again. He didn't want the disappointment of finding that she was only asking because she was well-mannered or – worse still – for the novelty value of spending time with the oddball.

Not that he thought he was an oddball, but he knew that other people saw him that way. He knew it was a result of his own insular existence, but what choice did he have really? It wasn't as if he could pretend that nothing had happened, because it had, and everybody knew it.

For now he opted to stay safely in the world of Tom Sharpe, whose boxset he had discovered buried in amongst the book pile. He was currently immersed in Porterhouse Blue and feeling glad that he had never got involved in academia, despite the great number of laughs it had elicited from him.

*

The patrol car was parked at the end of the pedestrian precinct. Wendy and Mark had just got back in, after an extended amount of time walking amongst the departing drinkers from the pubs and wine bars. Tonight had been good-natured, no arguments or brawls, just happy people having a good evening. They had stopped to talk to groups of young men and women, given directions to slightly tipsy pedestrians and chatted with the doormen on the route. A positive police presence, and some time to foster some good relations. Also some good suggestions from the doormen about who they might want to keep an eye on if they want to find out where the new drug influx was coming from. It felt like a good evening's work, even with no arrests or crises to report.

"So?" asked Wendy, "what happened?"

She was aware that the supermarket car park had been the focus of a lot of officers in the early hours of the morning, but as yet had not heard how it went. The fact that nobody had mentioned it to her made her think the mystery men had probably not turned up.

Mark looked at her.

"You don't know?"

"No, that's why I asked."

Mark's face broke into a smile and he laughed.

"Oh my settle back, you're in for a treat."

Wendy wasn't sure if this was in a good way or not, she nodded for Mark to continue.

"So, the boss decided we should act on the info straight away, in case they decided to change their meeting place. I'm sure you gathered that from all the extra bodies around yesterday, I think they called in every single officer in a hundred mile radius. I think most of them spent the night at the station drinking tea and being on call in case there was a need for backup.

They had the lot, dogs, plain clothes, drugs team, firearms officers, more people than you could shake a stick at. Steve Barclay, your boss – who's very helpful, reopened the store after everyone had gone home. The shelf stackers had to work around a bunch of coppers who were hunkered down at the back of the store where they couldn't be seen. He even laid on trays of doughnuts for them, stereotyping. Although, to be fair, I think they finished most of them off.

Cars and vans were way back in all the sideroads, a couple of unmarked at the back end of the carpark and the helicopter on standby. It was blanket coverage, very thorough, no chance we were going to miss them if or when they turned up."

Wendy had kind of guessed most of this, some of it was just standard procedure, some knee-jerk to the pressure to stem the new influx of drugs in town. She did not deny Mark the pleasure of his build up though, as he was clearly enjoying setting the scene.

"Anyway, both cars turned up, pretty much exactly like they did in that video you provided."

"Same cars?"

"Yep, at practically the same time. They got out and swapped the package, then the order to go came. They just stood there while the entire car park filled with squad cars, vans, dogs, coppers and every toy at the chief's disposal. They were good as gold, did everything they were told."

"So we got them then?"

"Well, yes, but I haven't got to the best bit yet." Mark's cheeks were already creasing as he tried to hold back on the smile that he knew would erupt into laughter before he was finished, he struggled on with the story.

"They were both local guys, one owns a restaurant, the other lives up by the woods. Turns out that the restaurant is quite high end and the other bloke has dogs that he's trained to sniff out things in the woods. The mystery package was a bag of truffles."

"Truffles?"

"Yes, a kind of gourmet thing that…."

"I know what truffles are, why were they doing that in the middle of the night?"

"Well, they both have to start early for their jobs, apparently this was the most convenient time and place for them."

"Shit, seriously? Am I going to be in trouble for causing all this fuss over some bloody cooking ingredients?"

Now Mark did laugh.

"No, you weren't to know, it was a good call. Not all operations have an outcome. Anyway, you still have brownie points from the saving the baby thing."

Nevertheless, Wendy was mortified that she had caused such a major commotion over what turned out to be nothing. Bloody truffles!

"I'm so sorry, everybody's going to hate me."

"Not at all, everybody's going to be quite pleased at all that overtime without having to actually do anything. Might be worth warning you though, there may be some teasing, so prepare yourself for that."

Wendy groaned to herself, she knew what teasing looked like in the station. It was hilarious when it was someone else, there was a real need for letting off steam sometimes in what could be such a high pressure job. She guessed she was going to have to brace herself for it and suck it up.

"Come on, you made a good call, it just didn't turn out to be what everybody – not just you – thought it was, you did well."

At the end of the shift Wendy went to her locker to put her equipment away, there in front of her locker door was a box of chocolate truffles with a smiley face drawn on a post-it-note stuck on the top.

Chapter 22
Same Again

Wendy sought out Tim the next day. He was wiping down some trolleys that had been caught in a sudden downpour, giving them a swipe with a rag he kept in his pocket. This was just to get the worst of the water off the parts that people would be most likely to need to handle. He was focussed on what he was doing and it took him a moment to realise who it was standing and waiting for him.

"Hold on, I'll just finish drying the seat then you can…oh, hello, Wendy."

"Hi, I didn't know that was one of your duties."

"It's not really, but you know, if a job's worth doing…"

"Absolutely, I'm sure people appreciate it."

"I hope so."

"Anyway, I didn't really come to talk about trolleys, are you still up for that drink you promised me? Or did you forget?"

Tim felt himself get warmer inside his waterproof and hoped his face didn't betray him. He hadn't forgotten of course, and it had been said in a non-accusatory manner, but still he felt guilty. He had convinced himself that the tentative arrangement had been made mostly out of good manners and now realised that maybe it hadn't.

"Ah, sure when would be good for you?"

"What about tonight? The Tailor's Thumbs, that's about half way between us?"

Tim didn't mind the Tailor's, it was usually not too crowded, more of a quiet drink place.

"Sure, eight o'clock?"

"Brilliant, see you there."

Wendy turned and walked back inside with a smile on her face. Tim watched her go, standing with one hand on a trolley and wondering if he could make himself look any stupider than he already seemed to have done. He was considering this when there was a light cough behind him, he turned.

"Is it okay if I take that?" a woman whose head peeked out of the top of her raincoat like a turtle politely enquired.

"Oh sure, sorry."

He passed her the trolley then continued about his business, still deep in thought.

*

"I don't know what to wear."

He had a selection of different clothes spread over the bed.

"God, I hope we don't end up wearing the same again, that would be embarrassing."

He held up a shirt against his body.

"Too fancy? Yeah, we're going to the pub, not the Ritz."

He put it back down and tried a grey jumper.

"This? God you're no bloody help are you?"

He decided it was the right mixture of smart and casual and put it on over a t-shirt.

"Of course you're no help, sorry. You've never been on a date have you?"

He didn't know if that made Ian unfortunate to have missed out, or lucky to not have had to go through the rituals and palaver. On balance he thought it was probably the former, he was pretty sure Ian would have enjoyed the whole dating thing, even though he hadn't.

"Anyway, it's not even a date, just going out for a drink."

He put away the unneeded clothes, leaving the room tidy once again. He had blitzed the house once he was done with the book mountain, tidying from top to bottom. Wendy had been his first visitor in a long time and the general clutter had been obvious to him, if not to her. He usually kept everything tidy, but recently he had let things slip as he had been spending more time than usual out of the house. Now he was back on track and the situation had been rectified, with everything in order and the cleaning caught up on.

"Right, I'm going out. Not a date, just a drink. I won't be late."

Even though it wasn't a date he still brushed his teeth and retied his hair before he left the house, walking the short distance to the pub. He looked around at the sparsely populated interior and, seeing that Wendy had not arrived yet, ordered a drink and settled at a table. He sat facing the door, so he could see when she arrived. This also meant he saw everyone else who arrived; two couples, one older and one younger. Both pairs lost in their own conversations, as a group of four cheerily loud lads who made a beeline for the pool table while one their group ordered drinks.

He was sipping his drink when Wendy came in, he immediately got up and offered to get her a drink.

"That would be lovely, thank you, white wine please."

"Sure thing."

He ordered the drinks and turned back to look as Wendy took her coat off, he froze when he saw that she was wearing jeans and a grey jumper. He finished paying and passed her drink while apologising.

"I'm sorry," he said, pointing at their jumpers in turn.

It took Wendy a moment to realise what he was apologising for, when she did her face broke into a huge smile.

"I guess I didn't get the memo this time either," she said with a laugh, "we'll have to make sure we coordinate properly on our next date. Or un coordinate I guess."

Tim relaxed a little, glad she didn't seem as horrified as he had felt. In fact, she seemed completely relaxed, which put him more at ease. In the past people had been reserved with him initially; the quiet guy, the trolley man, the oddball, the missing kid's brother. It always made things a little uneasy, which was why the first date was often the last. But Wendy had already mentioned their 'next date', which Tim supposed to mean that this was a date and not 'just a drink' and that there was a chance of another.

Less nervous now, the conversation started with small talk, work, the weather, books - a lot about books. Wendy commented on the full bookshelves in the house and Tim confessed that he had hidden most of the overflow before she arrived, and subsequently had a cull. Wendy confided that she had not read much at school, it wasn't what she and her friends did. In the last year or two, since she realised what she had been missing out on, she had been trying to find books that she would enjoy as much as some of the ones she had recently been discovering for herself, mostly on the back of TV programmes or films she had enjoyed. It had been a pleasant surprise to her how much richer the imagery, language and storytelling had been when you read it.

This was great for Tim, he found it easy to talk about his favourite books and stories, what he had been reading and what he had lined up ready. He surprised himself by inviting Wendy to come over again some time, to see if there was anything she might like on his shelves. Wendy surprised him back by agreeing enthusiastically, and even suggesting that it should be sometime soon – maybe later in the week.

As they started on their second drink, a rarity for Tim, Wendy broached the topic of the tape.

"They found out what was going on with those men in the car park, they set up an interception on Monday. The full works, with half the county's officers in on it."

Tim leaned forward, "You waited until now to tell me? What happened?"

Wendy explained about the highly unusual, but definitely not illegal, fungus trade that had been going on.

"Oh no, how awful that I put you to all that trouble for something innocent."

"No, you were right to show me, it looked dodgy as fuck, that's why they got onto it so quickly. Anyway, it wasn't all bad, the truffle man had his spaniel with him – the one he uses for finding the truffles. Apparently the canine unit's sniffer dog has a brand new best friend."

They both laughed at this, then Wendy added, "There was still something wrong with that video though, I just can't put my finger on it."

"So you think they may have been up to something?"

"No, it wasn't that. Something else, I don't know what, just something wrong."

They both sat in silence for a moment while they sipped their drinks, then conversation turned to Wendy's upcoming exams.

"I can help you revise if you like."

He wasn't quite sure why he said this, it wasn't as if he had any real experience with exams or revision.

"Would you? I might just take you up on that. I'm starting to get a bit nervous about the tests now they're nearly here."

"Of course, any time."

The thought of spending more time with Wendy gave Tim an odd feeling that he couldn't define; something between excitement and anticipation, which intensified when Wendy replied.

"I'm busy tomorrow, how about I come round the day after, I'll steal some of your books and you can ask me some police type questions?"

"Okay, that would be great, it won't be stealing though, you'll be welcome to them. Maybe I could cook us something."

The moment the words left his mouth he regretted them. Not the books and police bits - the cooking. He couldn't recall a time that he had ever cooked for anybody else, he was used to his own company and his own cooking. Too late now though, he'd offered.

"Oh there's no need to go to the trouble, we could just get a takeaway or something."

Tim let out a relieved breath, "Okay, it's a date."

They put their empty glasses back on the bar and moved outside where a solitary smoker was sitting at the single table that had been left out for that purpose.

"Walk you home?"

"No, I'll be fine, but thanks."

Tim looked around at the deserted street lit with the bright glow of the street lighting and blue yellow light from people's windows. Wendy saw him looking.

"It's okay, I'm only round the corner. I'll call a police officer if I get into trouble."

This brought a smile to Tim's face. He stood awkwardly for a moment, not sure whether he should attempt to give her a kiss - or if it was 'not that sort of date'. He shuffled slightly, starting to move in the direction that led towards home. As he started to turn Wendy reached out and took hold of his arm. He turned back to face her as she leaned forward and kissed him on his cheek.

"Thank you, I had a lovely evening."

"Me too, see you the day after tomorrow."

Wendy smiled and turned away from him, over her shoulder she called, "I'm looking forward to it already". Tim stood and watched as she walked into the night, absently putting his hand up to his cheek and holding it there before finally turning towards home when Wendy disappeared around the distant corner of the road.

She knew he was watching her go as she self-consciously strode along the pavement. She was beginning to wish she had let him walk her home now, not that she needed protecting – it just would have been nice to spend a little bit more time with him. Maybe she could even have invited him in for a coffee, she knows that's what younger her would have done.

But it didn't seem like the right thing to do tonight. She knew other people thought Tim was a bit simple, and for reasons she couldn't understand she thought that suited him just fine. His shyness had been evident from the first time she met him, painfully shy. Except that wasn't exactly it, he didn't blush or stumble over his words like people sometimes do when they feel awkward. Nor did he seem to find eye contact hard, it was something else, something she couldn't quite put her finger on.

Running over the evening's conversation, intelligent, witty and warm, but guarded. She had talked a bit about her own life but Tim had kept subtly diverting any potential discussion about him. It was adeptly done, inconspicuous – which was ironically what had made her eventually notice it. Whatever his reasons, she was sure he had them, she was just happy that she was going to be seeing him again soon.

Chapter 23
Replay

The evening was going well so far. Wendy had turned up in a grey hoodie, so they had not spent the evening looking like Tweedle Dum and Tweedle Dee, although that had not been entirely accidental. Before she arrived Tim had put a selection of different sweatshirts and jumpers on his bed, in assortment of colours and styles. This had included a grey hoodie as a possible option, but by waiting at the upstairs window he was able to see what Wendy was wearing before she arrived. He quickly selected a striped top for himself, then put the other clothes away rapidly and went downstairs ready to answer the door.

Of course, this meant that the general cleaning and tidying had needed to be done well in advance, everything tidy, nothing too obviously in need of a good scrub – including himself. The bath had been deep, hot and relaxing, the perfect place to mentally prepare for Wendy's visit, which he was now almost 100% sure counted as an actual date.

"I think she likes me, I like her. I just don't know what I'm going to tell her about…. well, you know? About everything."

He had been surprised that she hadn't asked about his brother yet, most people bought the subject up fairly early on. Although some people made a point of never mentioning it at all, which made it even more conspicuous – the proverbial elephant in the room.

"It's like she hasn't mentioned it because she doesn't know, but it was all over the TV and news, so how could she not? She's only a couple of years younger than me."

He thought about it for a moment.

"If she doesn't know, should I tell her?"

This was a new train of thought for Tim, he had never had to tell his story to anybody before, the local community were all too familiar with it, and the gossip machine was always ready to leap into action if this information needed to be discussed. When he was younger he would often find that conversations stopped when he walked into a room, and he knew that they had been talking about Ian. But not many people wanted to talk to him about it, and even if they did he wasn't sure he wanted to.

"I think I'll just wait and see what happens; she'll say something eventually."

He dried himself with the towel, wondering what Ian would have done. He'd tell Wendy for sure, he had always worn his heart on his sleeve. But thinking he knew what Ian would have done did not help him decide what he was going to do, so he fretted about it while he got dressed and finished tidying up.

In the end it hadn't been an issue. Wendy had bought a bottle of wine that they opened as they began to rifle through his cornucopia of books, talking about what would be good to read if you were in a certain mood, whose writing was reminiscent of another person's and how many it would be decent to borrow at any one time. In Wendy's words she 'didn't want to have to bring a wheelbarrow every time she came'. The last issue was resolved by the creation of a discrete pile that Tim would keep to one side for Wendy to swap from whenever she came round. Not least because he liked her presumption that she would be coming round again.

They finished the book hunt when their curry arrived, stopping to eat and realising that they had over ordered. Neither of them being used to ordering for more than one person, they had overcompensated and before long were sat looking at a collection of dirty plates and half-empty foil cartons.

"Well, how about I tidy up and then we can do some of your revision?"

"I'll help tidy, it's partly my mess."

"No, it's easier if I do it, I know where everything goes. Go into the sitting room and I'll bring you a cup of tea in a minute."

"You've talked me into it, I'll just pop up and use the loo first if that's okay?"

"Sure up the stairs, second on the left."

As he packed everything away and piled the leftovers into the fridge, Tim decided that now was the time. Before they started looking at Wendy's police books he would tell her about his brother, best to get these things out in the open. He heard her come down the stairs as he was boiling the kettle and before long joined her bearing two steaming mugs.

Wendy was not looking at her text book, it lay unopened on the coffee table. She was also not perusing the bookshelf, she was standing by the sideboard where Tim had left the camera after the last time he used it. She was turning it around in her hands and looked up guiltily as he came in.

"Sorry, not being nosey, I just saw it there."

"No worries, I think you've seen everything on it anyway."

"Can I watch it again?"

Tim was a bit taken aback, this wasn't what we had expected. He could think of no reason not to apart from the fact that it was just a video of two men trading mushrooms.

"Sure, I'll plug it into the TV. Here's your tea, have a seat."

  He attached all the cables and switched the TV set on then pressed play.

The camera panned around the kitchen, then zoomed in and out several times on the dimly lit, empty, car park.

"Oh, it's all the test bits again, do you want me to fast forward?"

He was already reaching for the camera when Wendy said "No, leave it, it's okay".

It pans across the car park, tracking a young couple who enter the station.

The car drops off the man with the suitcase.

People come out of the station, two young lads, the male half of the couple who went in earlier and someone who seemed a bit the worse for wear.

Two women getting out of a car.

The young lads from earlier returning to the station.

A group of friends fussing around, and bidding farewells as some of them went into the station and the others drove away.

The scene changed to the supermarket where a learner driver is hopping around in large, uncertain circles.

It stops again, then a fox walks into view.

"Can you rewind it?" Wendy asked.

"Sure, where to?"

"The start, I want to see it again."

Tim rewound it to the beginning, pressed play and they watched the whole sequence again. And again, and again.

"There's something there, it's right in front of me and I just can't see it."

"Take a break, sometimes it helps to stop thinking and let your brain work for a moment."

Wendy laughed, she knew what he meant. They drank their tea and Wendy nudged the training manual with her foot.

"I don't really feel like looking at this tonight, do you mind?"

"Not at all, I was kind of dreading it. I've never been much of a one for exams really."

"You would have had all the answers though."

"I know, but even so I can feel the pressure."

"Okay, so let's not revise." Wendy slid marginally along the sofa, so their hips were touching and leant slightly into him.

"We can just sit and talk, that would be nice."

Tim stiffened slightly, then relaxed. Okay, this was it, he was going to tell her. He took a deep breath, she smelt of something flowery, a faint and strangely comforting smell for reasons that he couldn't explain. He composed himself, then opened his mouth to speak. But before he could say a word Wendy sat upright abruptly.

"Play the tape again."

Flustered for a moment, Tim regained himself, rewound the tape and played it from the start.

"It's them," Wendy's voice rose in volume and pitch, "those lads. Why did they get off the train and then straight back onto the next one? Play it again."

Tim did as he was told and Wendy leant forward, scrutinising the TV as closely as she could.

"Maybe they were just popping into a shop, or meeting a friend," Tim ventured.

"No, look, watch it again."

Wendy had the controller now and rewound the tape then played it again.

"Right, here they are getting off the train. See the taller lad in the dark track suit? He's carrying a bag right?"

Tim saw he was, a large holdall slung over one shoulder.

"Now look," the boys walked back into the station.

"It's gone, maybe they were just dropping it off for someone," Tim suggested.

"No, look, they've got a different bag now."

It was true, the shorter lad was now carrying a backpack that he hadn't had on the way off the train.

"That's it," Wendy was almost shouting now, "they're delivering something I'm sure of it." In the back of her mind she thought it might be where the drugs influx was coming from, although she had also thought that about the truffle man. She realised that she couldn't go back to Crowley with this, she was still smarting from the last drugs bust that she'd instigated. She sat back in the settee quietly, staring at the frozen image of the men walking back into the station.

"What do you think they're up to?" asked Tim.

"I don't know, but I'd sure like to find out."

"Can't you just tell them at the station and let them figure it out?"

"Um, maybe not after last week. I need to think of a different way."

They both sat quietly for a moment, lost in parallel trains of thought. Finally Tim broke the silence.

"They didn't get a taxi."

"Hmm, I know, I saw that."

"So they must have walked to wherever they were going."

"Yes...." Wendy was starting to catch up with what Tim was thinking.

"And they had to walk back again, so wherever it was it has to be close to the station."

"Still, it could be anywhere."

"It could, but look."

Tim put his finger on the screen, pointing to the bottle in the tall lad's hand.

"It needs to be somewhere he could get a drink, close enough to walk to from the station and, presumably, where he could meet someone."

"So, that's the…"

"Supermarket." They both said this last word at the same time, looking at each other and smiling. As Tim sat back down Wendy leaned across and kissed him on the cheek, he turned to face her and she kissed him again, this time on the mouth. Tim froze, he needed to tell her, had to let her know what she was letting herself in for. Or find out if she was just messing with him, like previous girlfriends had.

She pulled back.

"I'm sorry, was that okay? I was just overexcited, tell me if you don't want to."

Tim looked into her green eyes and felt something he hadn't felt before, something that had been missing, and he wanted it. He decided the discussion about Ian could wait for another day.

"It's fine, it's nice, just…unexpected, sorry." He leaned towards her, then suddenly stopped. "If it is the supermarket Ahmed will have CCTV, we can see if they do go there. If they do, we may see who they meet."

"We'll ask him tomorrow shall we?"

Tim abruptly got up to make more tea. Wendy wondered if she had made a mistake, misread the situation. She was enjoying getting to know Tim, even though he had still not divulged much about himself. Maybe she had just been moving a bit too quickly for him, she decided she would slow down.

When she left Tim offered to walk her back, or call a taxi. She declined both offers, wanting the time to clear her head and think. They both thanked each other for a lovely evening, kissed one more time on the doorstep, then parted.

"Tomorrow then, we'll nab Ahmed and ask if he's got the tapes still."

"Okay," agreed Tim, "just let me know when you and him are free, I can take my breaks whenever."

Tim went back inside, leaning back against the closed door. He could still smell Wendy on his clothes and taste her on his lips, he closed his eyes and savoured the moment. Finally he pushed himself forward and walked back into the house.

"I think she likes me," he called up the stairs, "if not she did a good impression. She knows about you, I'm sure she does, she just doesn't want to talk about it."

Before she had left he had seen her looking at the photos on the *mantelpiece*, all old and faded. One of the whole family in best clothes smiling in front of a grey studio background. The other was of Tim and Ian on the beach, looking like sandy peas in a sun-soaked pod. She had not asked about the pictures or the people in them, and this had persuaded Tim to believe that she was aware of his history. He knew the questions would come eventually, and that they would be hard when they did – as they inevitably were. But for now he was grateful that she had not made her brother a part of their budding relationship.

Chapter 24
Partners

The three of them clustered around the monitor in the small back room, the one where Ahmed sat with shoplifters while they waited for the police to turn up.

When they had asked him if the videos were still saved from the evening on Tim's video he had answered immediately.

"Yes, it's the same day those bloody kids came in again, you know, the pick 'n' mix bandits. I've saved all those clips for the police, not that they do anything. No offence." He nodded politely at Wendy as he finished speaking.

"None taken, can we look at the tapes? We're looking to see if a couple of guys came in here."

She told him roughly what time they would have been in and together they went into the backroom where he found the right place on the machine. Wendy described the men they were looking for and they watched the people entering the main doors.

"There, that's them." She pointed at the screen as the same two people from Tim's video walked into the shop. They were followed, seconds later, by the group of kids that had been eluding Ahmed for the last few months. The bandits. Wendy asked to watch a bit further, eventually the boys, she could see now that was what they were, 13 or 14 years old, came back out with the same change of bags they had seen on their own tape. They were followed soon after by Ahmed and a scattering of running kids with hoods up.

He stopped the recording and they all sat in a pensive silence, eventually broken by Ahmed.

"Do the police need this tape?"

"Not yet I don't think, it's just weird is all. Can we see what they do when they're inside?"

"To an extent, I'd have to fiddle around with it a bit. Do you want me to do that?"

"Yes, please, Ahmed, that would be interesting – to see what they do with the bag and who they meet with."

They all watched as the camera angles were switched expertly from one place to another, tracking the boys as they moved through the store."

"There's no coverage in that part of the store," said Ahmed, as they got to the far corner. They watched and waited until they reappeared a couple of moments later, with the smaller backpack.

"No coverage there at all?" asked Wendy.

"No, I've told management, it's on their list of things to do. Has been for ages. I don't think it's very far up the list to be honest."

While they had been talking Ahmed had absently tracked the boys as they stopped to get some drinks and sweets then made their way to the checkout then back out of the store. They all sat looking at the monitor, not sure what to do next. Tim finally spoke up;

"Have you kept the recordings of all the bandit raids?"

"You bet, I'm determined to catch those little bastards. I'll get them in the end."

"Do you think they're connected?" Wendy asked.

"Maybe, no, I don't know – it was just a thought really."

Ahmed caught on.

"Do you want me to look back through the recordings and see if those lads come in at the same time?"

"Would you mind?" asked Wendy.

"Not at all, it's good to have someone else looking at it. They've been the bane of my life. I'll have a look now and get back to you later if you need to go back on shift."

Wendy glanced at her watch and realised that she did need to get back, she hastily arranged to meet Ahmed again at the end of her shift and they went back to their respective jobs.

She found Tim in the car park on her way out, hurrying over to him waving a piece of paper.

"I've got it, all the dates. Ahmed checked all of it. They come to the store at the same times as the bandits, every time. I'm on shift tonight, what time do you start tomorrow?"

"I'm on an early, but I can swap it easy enough. I'll just stay later tonight."

"That's great, come round mine for breakfast and we'll look through it together. Is that okay?"

"Well, I don't know where you live." Also, he had not been invited to anybody else's home for years. Although he could or should have anticipated it, the thought hadn't crossed his mind. Wendy pulled a face and slapped herself on the forehead before giving him her address, setting a time of nine and hoping she would not oversleep. Not that it was likely, she was usually an early riser anyway, she wanted to go through the information Ahmed had given them and she was really looking forward to meeting up with Tim again.

At home that evening Tim busied himself looking through his clothes, trying to second guess what Wendy would be wearing tomorrow and avoid a clash. He finally settled on a black hoodie over a white Vans t-shirt, figuring that the two opposites give him a good chance. He could either zip the hoodie up or take it off as necessary.

"I've decided what to wear," he called into the other room, "I got some bagels and some croissants from the reduced section before I left, which shall I take?" He thought for a moment then continued, "I'll take them both, it's always good to have a choice."

With that he went back to his computer to finish the job he had started earlier. He had a hunch, but he didn't want to say anything until he was more certain. Mostly because he didn't want Wendy to think he was stupid, but also because he was so unsure about it himself. He would have to wait until tomorrow when he saw Ahmed's notes before he committed himself.

All the activity, intrigue and investigating reminded him of when, with Ian, he would cycle off into the local neighbourhood looking for adventure.

They had both read all of the Secret Seven books from cover to cover, and had convinced one another that there were mysteries afoot and plots to be foiled in their own neighbourhood. They hunted in vain for a suitable villain to catch or person to rescue, possibly even treasure to unbury, but to no avail. Eventually they had hit on the ingenious plan of creating their own mysteries to solve.

As will often happen with small boys, there was a major failure of communication. The original plan had been that one twin would go around the neighbourhood creating mysteries for the other to follow on and solve. Due to an unfortunate breakdown in their planning, in the excitement of the idea, they both thought that they were the setter. Each brother spent an entire morning separately moving garden ornaments, writing cryptic messages in chalk and relocating any object that was portable enough to be hidden.

Amazingly, they did not come across one another once during the course of the morning. They met over a sandwich and some squash at the kitchen table, both grinning from ear to ear. As their lunch disappeared their joint realisation that something had gone wrong began to dawn.

"But I thought that..."

"No, we said that..."

"Well, I thought..."

As they finished their lunch the first ring on the doorbell chimed through the house, followed shortly afterwards by a phone call and an angry neighbour. In one morning they had managed to turn themselves from being crimefighters to fugitives. Fugitives who had to spend the rest of the day sorting out the mayhem they had created and apologising to the people they had upset.

That was Tim's first and last experience of law enforcement, apart from assisting the police in their search for his brother. Neither event was an unqualified success, so he had some trepidation approaching this investigation, although it did feel good to have a partner in crime again.

Chapter 25
Planning Meeting

Bollocks. Wendy wasn't wearing a white or a black top, she had opened the door in a red tee shirt, which would have been okay – except it was a Vans tee shirt. With his hands full of bagels and croissants Tim was not able to zip up his hoodie and instead just had to laugh along with her when she noticed. He supposed it was quite funny really, even if part of him was mortified.

He was invited in and he proffered the assorted baked goods as he stood inside the front door of the flat. Wendy took them graciously and directed him towards the kitchen, which was as ruthlessly tidy and organised as the entrance hall had been. He wondered again what she had made of the slapdash tidy up he had performed in his own house. He took in the clear surfaces, matched cutlery hanging on its rack, neatly stacked glasses and mugs and a pile of familiar-looking books on the kitchen table.

On top of the pile was To Kill a Mockingbird, Tim picked it up and saw that the bookmark was already tucked a third of the way in.

"How are you getting on with Scout then?"

"She's adorable, I'm so glad you told me to read this one first, I'm loving it."

"I think I suggested it, not told you."

"Whatever, same difference, you were right. How does…"

"Ah uh, strictly no spoilers, you have to find out yourself or it's no fun."

"You're right, of course. Tea and a toasted bagel?"

Once the drinks and food were ready they sat down at the table and Wendy spread out the sheet of A4 paper that Ahmed had given her, smoothing against the creases to make it lay flat.

"I looked, it just seems to be random. But as far as Ahmed could see, those boys bought in a bag on every occasion that the bandits came in causing chaos, which nobody would have noticed because there was so much else going on."

Tim studied the list thoughtfully, tracking down it with his forefinger.

"See, I don't think there's any pattern to it do you?" asked Wendy.

"Hmm, not sure, hang on a moment." He withdrew a notebook from his own pocket, opened it and started to compare the two separate lists. Wendy did not interrupt as he closely scrutinised them. Finally he leant back and smiled at her.

"What? What is it? Come on, don't leave me hanging like this."

"It's a pattern."

"How? What's in your book?"

"It's the train times. I checked which train they had come on that night I filmed them. It was from Birmingham, the slow one."

Wendy realised that this should have been one of the first things she should have checked. So much for her being an aspiring police officer.

"So I looked at the timetables, you'd think that the slow train from Birmingham would come at the same time every day, but it doesn't. These are the times, and they match Ahmed's."

Wendy skirted around the table and hugged Tim before he realised what she was about to do, he soaked up her praise as she celebrated this surprisingly small achievement.

"Of course, we still don't know which days they'll come, only which train they use when they do. We don't even know what they're actually up to. What do we do now?"

Wendy picked up his list of train times, scrutinised them, then smiled.

"We have a stake out of course. We'll wait by the station at these times, if they get off the train we follow them, if they don't we go home – or go and get something to eat, or go for a drink. Whatever. If we try enough times we're sure to see them eventually. And if we don't, we get a chance to go out somewhere. Win, win."

"I think that's a plan I can get behind. Do we have to do it together? We could cover more of the times separately."

"Now where would be the fun in that? If I'm going to be a spy, standing outside a cold station in the dark, I want someone to talk to while I'm doing it."

Her eyes locked with Tim's and she reached across the table for his hand, he took it and she squeezed gently. He didn't say anything, just held on and looked at her.

"What's up? You look worried."

"Nothing, it's just that I haven't… well, what I mean is, you know. This is all a bit…"

Inarticulate as his response was Wendy understood it, she kept hold of his hand and smiled what she hoped was her most reassuring smile.

"I get it, you don't spend a lot of time with other people. No pressure, just let me know if I'm talking too much or getting on your nerves."

"No, it's not that, everyone thinks I'm weird, I'm the local freakshow."

"I don't think everyone knows you, you're just quiet. Quiet is nice, I like that."

Tim thought she was wrong, most people did know him. He wanted to ask her if she knew, to find out if he was just a project. But seeing the earnestness on her face stopped him asking the question, he smiled back and simply said, "Thank you. I like you too, it's good talking to you."

"You're welcome, more tea?"

Mugs refreshed, they sat and decided which would be the best times for them to start their sleuthing. A scribbled list sat between them, Tim looked up from it, "Like the Secret Seven, but two of us, three if you include Ahmed."

"Closer to the Famous Five really then."

"Yeah, but Secret Seven were better."

This was the start of a longer ongoing discussion about the relative merits of the two opposing groups of mystery solvers. Wendy had read a pile of Famous Five books she had found in the loft at her parents' house. Neither would surrender their own viewpoint about which group was best, finally deciding that whichever it was they needed a different name for just the two of them (three if you counted Ahmed). No decision was reached before the time came when they both needed to get on with what was left of their day. They arranged to meet at the station the following evening, with a tentative arrangement to go on somewhere else afterwards, if the two lads were a no show.

Chapter 26

The Famous Two

Most stations come equipped with somewhere to sit and wait outside the main building, a bench or two or some low walls surrounding flower beds that seem to survive with the minimum of maintenance. Tim selected a bench and settled down to wait, keeping a look out for Wendy while he sat.

From his vantage point he could see a part of the fence that was newer than the rest, repaired, repainted and reinforced. Years ago this had been a tucked away stretch of rusty chain-link, with a discrete space to park your bikes while you snuck through the gap at the bottom. It had been on his and Ian's regular route of places to visit, making sure they were unobserved before crawling under.

Once inside the barrier they could quickly move along to a small area of bushes and shrubs, from where they would be invisible. Having learned how to tell if a train was approaching from watching westerns, they would take it in turns to crawl out and put their ear to the track, listening for humming and vibration. It was all a bit academic, as you could clearly hear the train approach long before it reached their hiding place.

Some trains arrived at a leisurely pace as they slowed in a squeal of hot metal and diesel fumes before stopping at the station. These trains were the ones that Tim and Ian would get to squash pennies for them. Carefully placing them on the track before the locomotive arrived, then retrieving the flattened disc of metal once it had passed. Although they ceased to be legal tender at this point, they became far more valuable as playground currency, being traded for anything from football cards to marbles.

The faster through trains had a tendency to flip the coins in random directions, obliterating them or making them impossible to locate afterwards. But they had a different purpose. The express trains flew past at an impossible speed, shaking the bushes and creating a rush of wind, noise and hot air that could pull the breath from your lungs. Tim and Ian would wait for their approach, standing as close to the trackside as they dared, feeling the weight of the passing train as it thundered on to its final destination. Dust and grit would whip around Tim's eyes, making them water. He remembered looking across at Ian and wondering if the dervish with his arms outstretched and head thrown back was what he looked like in that moment. Laughing, with their hair and eyes wild, they would hurry back to their bikes then cycle to the end of the road, where a hill steeper than the side of Everest would help them recreate that feeling of speed and power as they raced each other to the bottom. Tim hadn't been back to the trackside since Ian went, even if his movements hadn't been so closely monitored it wouldn't have been any fun by himself. It just became another lost fragment of his childhood.

Wendy arrived five minutes before the train was due, waving as she approached across the car park. Tim could see her smile from the moment she first came into view and spotted him, he returned it with what he hoped was a reflection of her radiant beam. She sat next to him, lowering herself onto the bench, then she reached over and pulled down the zip on his jacket and looked inside. She immediately started laughing, causing Tim to look quizzically at her until she pulled open her own jacket to reveal a blue sweatshirt, practically the same shade as the jumper he was wearing.

"Shit, seriously?" he asked aloud, making Wendy laugh even more.

He zipped his jacket back up and looked at his watch. "Five minutes," he announced.

They waited without conversation, watching the station entrance even though they knew it was not yet time. They observed the increasingly frequent comings and goings wordlessly until, spot on time, the Birmingham train arrived. They both leaned forward and scrutinised every passenger that came out of the station, waiting until the last person had left the area. Tim sat back and let out a long breath.

"Drink then?" asked Wendy.

"Why not?" replied Tim.

They got up together and started walking in the direction of the closest pub, appropriately named The Railway Tavern, "Sorry about the sweatshirt," Tim mumbled as he took his first swallow of his drink. This caused Wendy to laugh again, saying;

"Don't apologise, I think it's funny. Maybe it's an omen."

"Of what?"

"I don't know really. Maybe it means we're in a secret club – like the Terrific Two or something."

They both laughed at this.

"I'm not sure, I don't think she would have approved of the brave heroes of her stories going to the pub."

"I'm sure the swarthy foreigners would be in here though, plotting their fiendish plans."

"Yeah, it didn't age well did it?"

They both drank some more and agreed that maybe they wouldn't be some kind of Enid Blyton tribute club. They made arrangements for the next stake out then Tim walked Wendy home, lingering for an awkward moment over his goodbyes before turning into the dwindling daylight and making his own way home.

Wendy closed the door and sighed before going to make some coffee and take her police manual to bed for some night reading. She promised herself that she would swap it for another chapter of Harper Lee before she went to sleep.

In the end she didn't really focus on either book as her thoughts kept turning to Tim. She was happily single, focussing on herself and her own needs for a change, or had been before the thing with the trolleys had happened. Now she found herself wanting to spend more time with him, he was quietly funny, ridiculously introverted and – she had to admit – very good looking. She had got the feeling that he liked her too, although he was clearly too shy to say or do anything. At the same time, there was so much she didn't know about him. He hadn't really talked about himself that much and she hadn't liked to question him too hard, not wanting to make him even more uncomfortable than he appeared to be already.

She guessed that he had been in a relationship previously, he was clearly fully domesticated, with no slovenly bachelor habits on display. Also, she had seen a child's bedroom made up when she had used the bathroom in his family-sized house. Most likely for the occasional visit from a son he shared with an estranged spouse. It was just odd that he never mentioned him, maybe he really didn't see him that often. She didn't see that as being a dealbreaker for starting a relationship.

It was altogether too much of a conundrum for her to try and work out for now. She was looking forward to the next time they would meet at the station and decided she would ask some more direct questions, to try and find out a bit more about his past and see if she could get him to open up a bit. For now she was just happy to know that she was going to get to spend some more time with such a kind and gentle man.

Her own father had been aloof, working long hours and spending time out with his friends drinking or watching football when he was off the clock. She had always had the feeling that he would have been happier if she had been a boy, but she wasn't and she always felt that her gender had been one of the main reasons he had eventually left. Her mum had not seemed surprised at the time, she had merely taken down his photos, got rid of the belongings he hadn't collected and got on with her life without him. It hadn't occurred to Wendy at the time that this was maybe a show of stoicism for her benefit, to help her cope with the loss of a dad she felt she barely knew. By the time this occurred to her, in her late teens, it felt as if too much time had elapsed to broach the subject. It became just another thing that her and mum didn't speak about.

She slept, and dreamed about being in a small gang of kids solving mysteries on an island that they reached by means of a small red rowing boat. Tim was, of course, part of the gang, along with Mark and Sergeant Crowley. The narrative was as obscure and nonsensical as dreams tend to be, but it left her with a warm, safe feeling when she awoke the following day.

Chapter 27
Happy Birthday

The following two meetings at the railway station were unsuccessful, both for spotting the lads with the bag and spending time together. The first time was before she went on to her shift as a special, she had been slightly relieved that the boys hadn't turned up as it might have delayed her arrival for work. Also, she wasn't sure how easy it would be to inconspicuously follow someone, who may be up to no good, in a police uniform. She had rushed off afterwards, promising to speak to Tim soon, although she had only had the briefest conversation with him after that, to confirm their next meeting. She had been hitting the Police Training Manual hard, hoping to assimilate some more of the information it contained before her impending exams.

She had thought they would have more time to talk the next time, maybe another drink afterwards if the boys weren't on the train. But Tim had seemed distracted, making conversation difficult as he asked her to repeat things she had said, delayed his responses and appeared to find it hard to initiate any discussions. He had apologised, apparently aware of his own social shortcomings, saying he needed to rush away once they had confirmed it was another no show.

Wendy was left bemused, she had been sure they were getting on well, and didn't think this was a 'treat them mean, keep them keen' ploy. She had asked if everything was okay, but had decided not to pry once he had assured her it was fine. She mostly hoped she hadn't been too pushy or forward, she ran back through their previous meetings in her mind and decided that it was probably not her. Which left her puzzling about what it could be.

Tim had returned home, going upstairs to sit on the end of the bed in his brother's room where he unwrapped a small parcel he had picked up from the kitchen table.

"Happy birthday." His voice was small and quiet, he kept his eyes on the Nirvana CD he had just unwrapped.

"I thought you'd like this, it's really good. I know you like loud music, so I thought this would be just the thing." He knew this because he liked loud music, and although they disagreed on some things, they had never not seen eye to eye where music was concerned.

"I'll put it on in a minute, rattle the windows. I know you're going to love it. I've got some cake downstairs, not a big one like mum always used to make, but you have to do something don't you?"

He sat quietly for a moment, then went back downstairs and put the music on as loud as he could tolerate before sitting in the armchair and leaning back with his eyes closed, letting the music wash over him.

Birthdays had been confusing, an annual reminder that Ian wasn't there. Mum had felt it intensely and had downplayed the event to the extent that it was barely acknowledged. While he was at home Dad had celebrated in his usual way of going to the pub and not returning until long after Tim's bedtime. Tim had decided that it should be a day to quietly remember his lost twin, at the expense of his own celebrations. Every year without fail he would get a card and a gift for Ian, these were piled carefully in the wardrobe, ready for when he came back. Over the years it had become a ritual, but Tim's intention had been that Ian would know that he had never forgotten him or given up hope, because sometimes hope is all you have.

Their last birthday together was when they got their bikes, the same bike that Ian had ridden to the park that day. Their old ones had been used so much they were falling into chronic disrepair, not to mention being so small that their knees reached the handlebars. Their delight when they came downstairs to find them in the kitchen had been intense, both of them sitting on their respective bikes in their pyjamas in the kitchen while they precariously ate bowls of cornflakes and talked excitedly about the adventures they would have.

They pleaded to be let out, to try their new bikes, drop handle-barred, razor seats and skinny tyres. Two racing bikes identical aside from the red and blue paint covering them. The colours had been allocated by a simple system of 'whichever colour you unwrapped was yours', neither of them minded, all they wanted to do was get outside and cycle.

Once Mum was happy that they were suitably dressed, washed and presented, with clean teeth and brushed hair, they were given permission to go, but only round the block or to the park, and home in time for lunch. They needed no further encouragement, the bikes were taken outside, mounted and pedalled furiously out of sight within minutes. There was no plan other than to enjoy the exhilaration of the freedom they would now enjoy. The block? The park? No, they had an unspoken common understanding that they would not be limiting themselves to those boring old places, they were going to explore.

They went through the park, past the 'no cycling' signs, and straight out of the far gate into uncharted areas. This was unfamiliar territory now; they had been this way before but only briefly and not very far. Emboldened by the euphoria of their new bikes and birthday excitement, they took it in turns to speed ahead of one another into various alleys, housing estates and arcades of run-down shops. Eventually Tim stopped, his brother squealing to a halt behind him.

"Why are we stopping?" asked Ian

"Which way shall we go now?"

"I don't know, do you know where we are?"

"Not really."

"Maybe we should start going back."

It was at this point that Tim realised that he didn't exactly know which way back was, they had criss-crossed over so many tiny roads and lanes that he was disoriented. None of the street names were familiar and he could see no landmarks that he recognised. The brothers looked at one another, each hoping the other would have a suggestion, then turned their bikes around and started to go back in what they thought might be the right direction.

Things got worse when they somehow managed to lose track of the various places they had passed on their way. Their best guesses and hunches did not deliver them to their starting point, in fact they ended up back in the same place they had stopped earlier.

"This is hopeless, we're lost," announced Ian.

Tim thought he was going to cry, but decided that if Ian wasn't then maybe he shouldn't either. Taking a big gulp he steadied his voice and said; "Maybe we could ask someone."

They both looked up and down the deserted street, then at each other. Suddenly Ian started to giggle for no apparent reason, once he had started Tim had to join in and soon they were both laughing out loud. An elderly man came round the corner and smiled as he passed them, making them laugh even more. He was a good 10 feet away when Ian suddenly realised that the man could be their saviour, he cycled to catch him up and politely asked the man if he knew which way it was to the park. They were pointed in a highly unlikely direction that was completely at odds with both their perceptions of where they should be going. Devoid of any other plan, they decided they might as well give it a try. The park was three streets away, less than a couple of minutes ride. They had evidently taken themselves in a big circle on their initial incursion into the territory, nearly back to where they started.

They cycled slowly across the park discussing their plans to properly explore and map the unknown territory in the near future. But for now they took their new bikes home, where they did not get told off for being late for lunch – because it was their birthday.

Over the years Tim had fully explored every square foot of the neighbourhood across the park in the hope of finding his brother – lost again. He had spent his time walking through the lanes, alleys, roads and streets looking for anything that might be a clue – maybe a chalked message on the pavement or a misplaced object. Always starting his forays at one or other of the park gates.

The town has grown in the intervening years, spreading itself through the surrounding countryside and joining up with smaller villages that used to sit outside its boundary. It was still not a large town, still not large enough to get lost – unless you're a small boy on a new bike.

Chapter 28

The Game's Afoot

Wendy had arrived early this time, she was waiting on the bench when Tim turned up and sat beside her.

"Sorry about last time," she said.

"What? Why?"

"I didn't mean to upset you."

"You didn't. It wasn't you, shit, I'm sorry if you thought that. It just wasn't a good day."

She put her hand on his, "Why? What was wrong?"

"Nothing, it's complicated. It's, well it was my birthday."

"No! You should have said, I'm sorry, I didn't know. We should have gone out and celebrated."

"No, I don't really do that on my birthday, it's just…it's not a good time for me."

Wendy wanted to ask more, to find out why Tim was so downbeat about what is a happy day for most people. But there was something about his expression that told her he had already reached his limit for disclosures for one day, that he had only given her that much information because he didn't want to talk about it.

A bedraggled pigeon landed on the pavement in front of them, pecking hopefully around in the optimistic anticipation of some food. She squeezed Tim's hand and looked at his face, eyes averted, slightly distant expression and vague other-worldliness. She was glad it wasn't her that had upset him, but decided that now would definitely not be the time to ask about his son. They sat in comfortable silence for a moment before Tim turned to her with an earnest expression on his face.

"I will explain, I just can't right now. Sorry."

"No problem, I'm here if you need me."

As she said it, she realised in that moment that she meant it. He seemed so vulnerable and lost somehow, not a project to be 'fixed' but a mirror to her own uncertainties and anxieties, why shouldn't they share their insecurities? She thought she would like that.

A taxi arrived, disgorging people and suitcases outside the station and heralding the imminent arrival of the train. They both watched as more people turned up, until they finally heard the high-pitched squeal of brakes as the approaching train pulled into the station.

"Do you want to come for a drink? A kind of non-birthday drink."

Tim did not answer, did not even appear to have heard as his eyes locked on the station entrance. She followed his gaze and saw the two boys walking out, one taller with bleached hair and a bag swinging lazily in his hand, the other walking beside him talking. It was the same as the video, they made a beeline across the car park and started walking in the direction of the supermarket.

"What do we do now?" Tim whispered.

"Follow them I guess, come on."

She got up and started walking, causing the pigeon to flutter away in alarm. Tim got up and started to walk alongside her. The boys did not look back, but Wendy realised that if they did, she and Tim would look as if they were doing exactly what they were doing. She reached out and took his hand again, slipping her fingers inside his and moving closer to him. He looked at her.

"We'll look less conspicuous like this, just two people walking to the supermarket together to get some cheese."

"Cheese?"

"First thing I thought of, I like cheese. Come on, pretend we're a couple."

They walked in silence, both of them considering what Wendy had just said. Each wondering separately if this little bit of make-believe was actually not so unbelievable. Tim broke the silence.

"What do we do when we get to the supermarket?"

"I haven't actually thought that through yet, I just want to see what they're up to really. Do you have any ideas?"

"No, I just thought that maybe you would. Or maybe it would be obvious. To be honest I didn't really think we'd see them."

"No, me neither. I guess we'll just have to play it by ear."

As they approached the car park a young girl appeared, walking up to the boys who stopped briefly to talk to her. Tim and Wendy slowed, she briefly considered kissing Tim to make it look more natural, but before she could the tall boy took something from his pocket, passed it to the girl and then carried on as the girl ran back to the shadows now pooling at the edge of the car park.

They arrived at the supermarket, walking through the door a few metres behind the boys. They didn't need to follow them now; they knew exactly where they would be going. Wendy paused to pick up a basket, as she did so Ahmed appeared at her shoulder and stage-whispered, "It's them boys, what do you want me to do?"

Wendy didn't know. She suggested he stay by the entrance and just be aware of what was happening - in case they needed his help.

"Don't bother chasing the pick 'n' mix bandits tonight, I think they're just the decoys."

Ahmed agreed and Tim and Wendy headed for the far corner of the store. They arrived in time to see the tall boy look around briefly then reach behind a pile of kitchen rolls and pull out a backpack, which he swiftly replaced with his own bag. The boys then turned and walked directly towards Tim and Wendy, who feigned deep interest in the battery display as they passed within a few feet of them – apparently oblivious to their purpose. Wendy waited until they had passed completely then turned to Tim.

"Come on then," she started towards the kitchen rolls, "don't you want to know what's in the bag?"

She took another step, but had hardly moved before Tim pulled her back by the hand, which he realised he was still holding.

"Wait, look," he nodded his head towards an older man in a hooded top and jeans who was looking around cautiously as he went towards the place the bag was stashed. As the man reached behind the rolls Wendy looked at him as surreptitiously as she could. She knew him, she was sure of it. She was good with faces and she definitely recognised his, with the droopy moustache and stubbly chin, she just couldn't remember where from. Then it hit her. It wasn't part of her current role to be involved in ongoing investigations, she was very much peripheral to what she thought of as 'real policing'. But when she had met with Sergeant Crowley the other day, they had walked through the ops room to get to his office. This man's face had been pinned on the board there, along with several others, in connection with the new influx of drugs and the attack on the elderly couple's house that she had been stationed outside some nights ago. She knew from the yellow sticker on the corner of his picture that he was currently wanted for outstanding warrants and questioning.

"Follow him," she told Tim, "I have to make a phone call."

Tim realised that Wendy had moved abruptly into a state of alert, you couldn't miss the dilated pupils, red cheeks and clipped way she gave the instruction. He didn't know quite what she had seen, but he didn't question her, merely followed her instruction. He tried to look casual as he walked after Mr Moustache, gazing at some of the objects on the shelves as he passed them, then speeding up as he walked out of the door.

While all this was happening the sound of shouting, laughing and things crashing to the floor started to echo around the aisles – the bandits were here.

As usual they created mayhem as they moved around the store, untroubled by Ahmed and free to roam at will. Tim heard something breaking, the noisy shattering sound resonating in the space as he left the store and walked across the car park. His instinct was to go back and investigate, make sure nobody was hurt, see if he could help. But he kept on task, maintaining a steady distance between himself and Mr Moustache who appeared oblivious to his newly acquired shadow. They left the parking area by the exit that led to the nearest housing estate, through an alley that made it impossible for Tim not to be directly behind the man. He paused when the man adjusted the strap of the bag and looked back over his shoulder, then breathed a sigh of relief when he turned and continued on his way, apparently not paying any mind to Tim. He got to the end of the cut through and turned left towards the flats as Tim hurried slightly in the hope of keeping him in sight when he got to the corner himself.

He came to the corner and stepped around and almost into the man with the moustache who had stopped and was standing facing him, he scowled at Tim and held up a wicked looking knife with a curved silver blade with a serrated edge on the back side.

"Have we got a problem?" he asked as he stepped towards Tim.

Chapter 29
Beaten

Tim was not a fighter, he had no experience of what to do in a situation like this. Like most people his first instinct was to run, just turn around and leave the area as fast as his legs would carry him. Also, like most people, he did not do this, he stood rooted to the spot while his mouth and brain attempted to work in conjunction to answer the question.

His wits slowly returned as the man repeated the question, this time more forcefully. Tim started to edge out into the road mumbling as he did so.

"No, I was just going, I was going to, uhm, over there," he pointed vaguely towards the flats and took another step around the angry moustache in the direction he had indicated. The man rotated his body so that he continued to face Tim, the knife still held in his hand with its tip pointing towards him.

Many years ago Tim had been convinced that he was an invincible warrior - along with Ian who had, obviously, watched David Carradine in Kung Fu with him the previous night. They went into the garden to practise their various punches and kicks on one another, pulling short at first but becoming more and more forceful as they both grew more confident in their martial arts ability. It was still within the realms of 'boisterous boy play' until Tim caught his brother's ear with a flailing arm at the end of an ineffectual spinning kick. Unbalanced, Ian fell on his backside with an undignified bump, then got up with fire in his eyes and a clear intent to get his revenge in spite of Tim's apology.

Scared for his own safety Tim did what any sensible person would do in a similar situation; he picked up an abandoned cricket stump and held it in front of him. This may have worked if there hadn't been another stump laying nearby, Ian appropriated it and then both boys circled one another looking for an opening to attack.

By the time their mum came and broke up the stick fight, both boys were bloodied and shouting angrily at one another. They were marched inside, patched up with plasters and Savlon and sent to sit in separate rooms for the remainder of the afternoon. By teatime they were desperate to get back together, to compare bruises and argue about who would have won if they had been allowed to complete their game.

He was pretty sure that had not prepared him sufficiently for being confronted with a knife wielding drug dealer, he continued to try and edge around and away from him as best he could. He was in flight or fight mode and was mentally getting himself ready to attempt the former option, right when Wendy came careening around the corner and the man spun fully around to face her with his knife now raised and ready to attack.

Wendy had arrived outside in time to see Tim crossing the last parking space, just before he would have been lost from sight. She had sprinted across the area, unmindful of moving cars and shoppers moving trolleys, and into the alley. There was still no sign of Tim so she continued to race through the semi-dark and around the corner where she was confronted with the bagman threatening Tim with a knife, and this made her furious.

"PUT THE FUCKING KNIFE DOWN!" she yelled, to the bemusement of the bagman who waggled the tip of the blade at her.

"I'll deal with you in a moment, bitch, I've got other business to sort out first."

He spun back to face Tim and lunged with the knife; instinctively Tim put his hands up and stepped back, feeling the tip of the knife snag his sleeve. He took another step back as Mr Moustache prepared to lunge again, when suddenly his assailant went flying to one side as the full force of Wendy screaming incoherently and barrelling into him, knocked him to the ground.

In this moment all Tim could think of was Wendy, she was up close and personal with a knife-wielding maniac and the only thing he truly knew in that exact moment was that he didn't want her to get hurt. Acting on nothing but instinct and hope he dropped his full weight on top of Mr Moustache, landing with his shoulder in the middle of the man's chest. He heard the breath whoosh out of his lungs in a drawn-out, barely coherent, obscenity and saw that Wendy was already back on her feet and had raised her foot to stamp on the hand holding the knife. It was not the kind of dramatic action sequence that he had tried to emulate with his twin all those years ago. It was a messy scuffle. Wendy had got him to release the knife; for her pains she had been grabbed by the ankle and pulled back over as their attacker attempted to get to his feet and regain his breath. Fists flailed. Tim felt one connect with the side of his face as he tried to roll away, and Wendy got knocked back over as she was halfway up again.

As Mr Moustache looked on the ground for his knife there was a sound from the alley, he looked up then clearly decided to cut his losses and run. As Mark appeared around the corner he shouted, "Stop, police!"

Mr Moustache started to run, clutching his bag to his side, and Wendy stuck her leg out from where she had last landed, tripping him and sending him sprawling. Before Tim had even really processed what was happening the fight was over.

Mark was putting handcuffs on the wrists of the prone man while simultaneously calling back over his shoulder, "Are you okay? Wendy, are you two alright? Is anybody hurt?"

They looked at each other from where they were both sitting on the ground a short distance apart from one another. Wendy had a trickle of blood coming from her nose. Tim's eye had already started to swell and close up. They both started to stand up and simultaneously noticed the blood dripping from Tim's sleeve, once he saw it Tim realised that it was hurting. He rolled his sleeve up to reveal a cut; small but bleeding freely where the knife had caught his arm.

Mark was already radioing for an ambulance and a van to their location, two more officers had arrived – one was helping Mark get Mr Moustache into a sitting position amid much bellicose swearing and threatening. The other was Lanky Pete who rushed over to Wendy.

"Wendy, oh my god, are you okay?"

She answered, in a slightly nasally voice, that she was fine and told Pete to get a dressing on Tim's arm. He immediately pulled an emergency pack from a pouch on his vest and started to wrap it around the cut on Tim's arm. Tim took it gratefully and held it in place, glad not to have to see the cut any more as the sight of the blood - oozing wound had been making him feel slightly queasy. The road quickly filled with the flashing lights of emergency vehicles, strobing red and blue in the dying light, and a morass of people - some serving an obvious purpose, others looking for a purpose to serve. Wendy was deep in conversation with Mark, who was listening intently and pausing to relay information over his radio at regular intervals, when Tim felt a tap on his shoulder.

"Hi, Tim, you've had an exciting afternoon."

It took Tim a moment, the man was older now and was sporting a beard and sergeant's stripes, but he recognised the voice as belonging to the young policeman who had been so kind to him all those years ago.

"Hello, George."

"How's your arm feeling? We're going to get you in an ambulance in a minute and get that looked at."

"Thanks. I hope I haven't got Wendy in trouble."

Crowley laughed, "Quite the opposite, you've probably got her a medal and she hasn't even joined us properly yet."

Tim felt some relief at this, he knew how mortified she'd been after the truffle incident.

"Anyway Tim, it's good to see you, although maybe not the best circumstances. We will want to get a statement from you sometime soon. I'm really looking forward to hearing how you got involved in this. I'll make sure I'm around when you come into the station if that's okay?"

"Yeah, that's fine."

A paramedic had arrived now and was hovering behind them, Crowley relinquished his position after clapping Tim on the shoulder and telling him he'd see him soon. He had an ulterior motive to wanting to be around of course, he had never fully let go of what was one of his first cases – or forgotten the scared, lonely boy that had been caught up in the middle of it. He wanted to make sure that Tim was treated with the respect and dignity that he deserved. Tim was already relieved to know there would be a familiar face, someone he felt he could trust, when he was being questioned.

Wendy and Tim shared the ambulance ride. She insisted on it. The paramedic had told Tim he would just need a few stitches and a dressing for his arm. Both of them had been told that they would need to have their head injuries checked before they would be allowed home.

Wendy pointed to his swollen eye then her own.

"Still twins then," she joked. There was a brief moment of slightly awkward silence, broken by Tim laughing out loud.

"I told Ian about how we keep dressing the same. It's really funny when you think about it."

"Ian?"

"Yes, I tell him pretty much everything."

From the offhand way he had been dropped into the conversation again Wendy felt that she should have known who Ian was; she assumed it was his son. This did not feel like the time or the place to ask as they pulled up outside the hospital and were escorted into

A&E. She reached out and held his hand as they went in; Tim squeezed it back and held it tightly until they were taken to separate bays to be stitched, cleaned and assessed. It was midnight by the time they were delivered to their respective homes by squad cars that had been detailed for that purpose.

Chapter 30
Now It Makes Sense

Wendy was back in Crowley's office; he had told her she didn't need to come in so early, but she had wanted to get her statement down while it was still fresh in her mind. Her eye was swollen shut and her nose hurt like hell in spite of the painkillers she had taken.

"We'll do this, then you need to go home and rest. I know I can't really give you orders yet, consider that a pre-emptive one for when I can."

"I will, I feel as bad as I look."

"You don't look too bad."

"Flattery will get you nowhere, and nor will lying."

"Okay, you look like shit. I've asked Mark to come in to take your statement, I hope that's okay."

"That's great, I need to thank him for last night."

"Before he gets here, give me an overview. How did you come to be in a back alley with a drug dealer waving a knife around? And how did Tim get dragged into all this?"

"You know Tim don't you?" She thought maybe their families knew each other, or that they had mixed in similar social circles at some point.

"Of course I know Tim, probably better than most."

"What? Other people here know Tim? Has he been in trouble?"

"Not that I know of. Seriously, do you not know who Tim King is?"

"He's the nice guy I work with and I've been kind of seeing."

"Okay, tell me about yesterday, then I'll tell you about Tim."

Wendy briefly explained about the video and how she and Tim had been intrigued, but that they hadn't wanted to bring it back to the station until they had an idea what it was. Then she had seen the man from the incident board and decided she needed to act. Crowley listened attentively, nodding but not interrupting, when she got to the end he let out a low whistling sound.

"You are quite the crime fighting duo aren't you? Good work, though I'm surprised nobody else picked up on that when they watched the video."

"It wasn't what they were looking for, we only found it by chance."

"Well, it was a good catch. At least we know how the drugs are arriving now, and where they're coming from. The two lads they picked up at the station have been most helpful."

"Good, now tell me about Tim."

"Ian King," Crowley answered looking meaningfully at her. There it was, that name - Ian. Wendy thought maybe it did mean something to her, but she wasn't sure what. She looked at Crowley and shrugged her shoulders slightly.

"Didn't you watch the news when you were a kid?"

As it happened, Wendy rarely did. Her authoritarian dad set strict limits on who could watch the TV and when, which mostly meant it was for him to watch Match of the Day and Some Mothers Do Have 'em. The rest of the time it was strictly controlled and out of bounds. What precious time Wendy could get access to it was usually reserved for pre-news shows that she could watch before he arrived home from work. She shrugged again.

"Okay, Google it, it'll make sense then."

Crowley's phone rang at that moment, leaving Wendy free to leave his desk and find a free computer in the main office. She logged on and typed 'Ian King' into the search bar, there was a pause then pages and pages of links opened up, a staggering number of articles, videos and news stories, all about Ian. She was overwhelmed by the mass of information that appeared on the screen, some of it now ringing a bell in the recesses of her memory. What had been indelibly imprinted on the public's collective consciousness had somehow managed to only faintly register for her.

As she read she became lost in the story; the retelling of how Ian had vanished and the ensuing search that had borne no results. She also read about the lonely twin who had been left behind and the efforts of the press to engage Tim in interviews, articles and stories. Tabloid nonsense thinly disguised as investigative journalism, but was sensationalist and offered no help to the investigation – a procession of lurid headlines and speculative stories with Tim's face, younger but still clearly recognisable, staring back at her. Everything about Tim started to make sense to her now; no son, just a lost brother and a life of loneliness. She realised with a strange feeling that he would have assumed that she knew all of this; he would have wondered why she never mentioned Ian and if that had been a relief or an insult. If neither of them, then what?

Crowley came up behind her.

"It was one of my first cases as a young copper, it nearly broke my heart. I hated that we never found him. I was his family liaison officer, only I never really had anything much to liaise about. I've kind of kept an eye out for Tim over the years, especially when the anniversary comes around or when another kid goes missing somewhere else. He was vulnerable for a while, especially when the family broke up. I think he's been on top of things since then, but I'm worried that this is going to be hard for him."

"Maybe, can't he just be kept out of it?" asked Wendy.

"Ideally, yes. The press have already got hold of the story, someone will make the link to his name – I guarantee it. I would have tried to keep it quiet, but someone didn't think about what they were saying.

Reporters aren't stupid, one of them will make the connection and try to use that as an angle to make their story different."

"Why? It has nothing to do with it."

"Because people like to read about that sort of stuff, any kind of disaster that doesn't affect them directly is a good read." Wendy made a disapproving noise as Crowley continued, "I'm not sure what kind of relationship you have with him, and it's none of my business, but I'm guessing he's going to need all the support he can get for a while."

Wendy understood, she thanked Crowley and collected her belongings ready to leave.

"Look after him, let me know directly if you need anything, and say hi from me."

Chapter 31

The Map

The map in his hand was frayed and creased, with several small tears and yellowing paper. After their birthday they had been more circumspect in their explorations. Of course, it had been Ian's idea to make a map of the places they visited, at least that was how Tim remembered it. Looking at the map now he could see that a lot of the writing was his neat printing, not Ian's clumsy right-handed scrawl, maybe Ian had just let him do it as he disliked writing so much.

Their house was at the centre of the map, with the surrounding roads neatly labelled. The route to the park was shown, along with the best way to get to the sweetshop with an arrow pointing in the direction of their school. Around the edge of the map were any places they had found that they deemed worthy of recording and directions on how to get to them – 'past the church', 'along the edge of the builders yard' and other specific instructions.

In the top left corner was an elaborate picture of an orchard they had found; it had been quite a ride to get there and the apples had been disappointingly small and green. They had planned to revisit at intervals until they were grown and edible, then to gorge on stolen fruit.
There was an avenue where half of the trees were conker trees; another place to earmark for future visits.

Further down the right hand side of the page was the stream, a small drawing of the bridge and stepping stones indicating its location. Tim remembered the days they had spent there 'fishing'. They did not bring home any fishes, but they did build several dams, bomb leaf boats from the bridge and roll their trousers up and paddle in the icy water. More than once they had slipped and fallen and gotten so wet they had to drape their clothes over the branches of the nearby bushes to try and dry them out before returning home.

The final part of the map had been the place where they had found the rope swing, through a gap in a fence at the edge of some abandoned buildings. It was an arching pendulum that swung out over a steep bank and reached its zenith a good twenty feet above the ground before returning to the top of the bank. Tim had left it too late to leap off and had ended up having to drop to the ground from a height greater than he was tall, his trousers ripped and knee bloodied he had rushed up laughing, ready for another turn.

What they didn't know then was just how accurate the map was. Although they had taken the centre of their world, the park, as the starting point rather than the middle of town, everything was positioned accurately, close enough to the actual compass points they would be on to make no difference. The park had been drawn at an odd angle that had put the main, north gate at the top of the page and everything else flowed from it. This had not been a conscious decision, but had nevertheless given them the chance to define the area they lived in. Or not, in Ian's case.

The addition of the rope swing had been near the end, one of the last things to be drawn carefully onto their map. For Tim it marked the end of the teeth-clenching, death-defying days of mud and blood. Shortly after the incomplete map had last been amended, the risks had been deemed to be too great, the dangers needed to be mitigated and Tim's world shrank to a safely controlled area of watchful adults.

He held it in his hand and lay down on Ian's bed, closing his eyes and waiting. He didn't know what for, he was just waiting, like he had spent his whole life waiting, wanting, wondering.

Chapter 32
Under Siege

The road was empty apart from the two men on the pavement, even from a distance Wendy could see their cameras dangling from their necks and realised that Crowley's fears had been confirmed and the press were after their story. As she approached one of the men noticed her, he peered intently then seemed to realise who she was and lifted his camera to start taking pictures. Instinctively she raised her hand to cover her face, not least because she didn't want to be photographed with her eye and nose swollen and bruised. They began to fire questions at her; questions about the drug dealer, questions about Tim, questions about Ian. She kept repeating 'no comment' as they pestered her and followed her up to Tim's front door.

As she knocked she turned to tell them to go away, to leave Tim alone. A dazzlingly bright flash temporarily blinded and disorientated her; she turned back and knocked again. As she did so she realised that the reporters had probably already tried this, Tim would think it was them again and be unlikely to answer. Unsure what to do now, she tried the door handle, more in hope than expectation. To her surprise it swung open; she stepped inside and closed it, leaning back against it with her eyes closed for a moment before moving forward into the house.

There was no sign of Tim in any of the downstairs rooms. Once she had finished checking them she started to walk tentatively up the stairs, calling quietly as she did so.

"Tim, it's me, Wendy. Are you up there?"

It occurred to her as she reached the top of the stairs that it was possible that Tim was suffering with a concussion after his blow to the head. The thought caused her to hurry on, where she saw that all the doors, bar one, opened onto dark and empty rooms. The closed door was the one where she had seen the child's bed on her previous visit, she opened the door and looked inside.

Tim was on the bed, curled on his side with his back to the door and what looked like a piece of paper clutched in his hand.

"It's me, Wendy," she whispered, "are you okay?"

There was no answer, she moved into the room guided by the light from the landing, looking down she saw that his eyes were open and staring into the corner of the room. Unsure what to do she acted on instinct, she put down her bag and climbed carefully onto the bed, wrapping her arms around Tim and holding him close. It felt good and it felt right, the warmth and solidity of his body leaned imperceptibly back towards her and wrapped itself deeper into her arms then started to shake. It was small at first, then started to grow as a keening sound came from Tim, a wild and haunting noise that she would never forget. She held him tighter and whispered into his long hair, telling him it was okay, that she was here, that she wouldn't leave him. As she told him this she realised that she meant it; if he wanted her she was his. She closed her eyes and started to sing softly, a song her mum had sung to her when she was small, and gradually he calmed and they both slipped into sleep.

It felt strange waking up in the wrong bedroom, disorientating for a moment. Tim had tried to move without waking her, now he stopped and rolled back to face her. Without saying anything he leaned forward and kissed her, gingerly to avoid their various contusions. She kissed him back as they locked in their embrace. Tim stopped and asked if it was okay, her answer was to pull him back for another lingering kiss.

Afterwards Tim looked to her and smiled.

"Thank you, thank you for coming."

"It's okay, I'm glad I did. Are you okay?"

He didn't look okay, but he certainly looked better than he had earlier. His eyes looked away from hers and he sat up on the edge of the bed, she moved herself until she was sitting next to him then indicated the room around them'

"I didn't know you know."

Tim looked at her astonished.

"You didn't know, really?"

"No, I thought you had a kid when I saw this room. Crowley told me about Ian today, I'm sorry."

"You thought I had a kid?" There was the suggestion of a smile and almost a laugh. "Crowley, he was alright, he tried to help."

"He said to say hi, he also said to ask if you needed anything. I'm going to call him later and see if he can persuade those reporters to piss off."

"That would be good, I've got nothing to say to them."

"Okay, do you want a cup of tea?"

"It should be me asking that, I'm sorry. Come on, let's put the kettle on."

They moved to the kitchen, where they were soon sitting at the table with steaming mugs in front of them. Tim looked across at Wendy, a questioning look that felt like she was being given a silent test, then he spoke in a voice so quiet it was barely there.

"I miss him. I miss him every second of every minute of every day. I wonder where he is and what he's doing. I know what the answer to that really is, but I like to imagine he's still around, still here with me. I can't bear to think of him any other way."

Wendy reached for his hand across the table and held it gently.

"I talk to him when no one else is here. I've saved all his things for him. Mum wanted me to throw it out, all of it, but I couldn't. Nobody else really knew what stuff was his and what was mine anyway, and everybody else was so busy grieving they just left me to get on with things. I hid his stuff in with mine. I put it all back into his room after Mum had died. I had to keep it, I couldn't manage without him."

There was another extended pause. Wendy waited.

"The worst thing is that everybody thought I was sad. I mean, I was sad, but that wasn't all of it." His voice was becoming louder and more animated now, "I was angry, angry that Ian didn't come back, angry that I was on my own, angry that I have to do this," he waved his arm in a circular motion that Wendy took to mean life in general, "by myself. I was angry that I hadn't gone with him that day, angry that he's never coming back – I know that, I've known it since he went – and most of all I'm angry because I don't know what happened to him. I just wanted to keep a little bit of him with me, keep a little bit alive, even though I'm angry with him."

He stopped, apparently having let out whatever he had been holding on to, and he looked at Wendy. She thought she would be out of her depth, but quickly realised that Tim wasn't seeking an answer, he had already heard the reassurances, advice and well-meant platitudes that could be offered.

"I get it," she whispered, tightening her grip on his hand. "I get it, it's okay."

"It's those reporters that did it, that's what brought it all back. I'm sorry."

"No need to apologise, but I am going to call Crowley right now and get them moved on, one way or another." She went to the house phone and called the now familiar number for the station, where she got put through to Crowley. After explaining briefly what was going on he told her not to worry about it, it would be dealt with as a matter of urgency.

"Have you got a back door?" asked Wendy.

"Yeah, there's a gate out to the lane."

"Come on then, pack some stuff up and we'll go to my flat until the reporters have gone. Mr Barclay has told us not to come into work this week, so we can hide out there."

Tim didn't argue or attempt to discuss it, he packed some underwear and toiletries into a backpack and showed Wendy the exit that he and Ian had used when they wanted to try and get out unseen by their mum. It had always seemed to work, but Tim realised when he got older that was probably because Mum was in on the scheme too. Anxious to give them their independence and freedom so they wouldn't think they were being babied. Tim often wondered how that decision must have felt to her in later years, although they had never discussed it.

It had occurred to Wendy, after she had made her impulsive offer, that she only had the one bed at her flat. She wasn't sure how to broach this with Tim, if she should offer it to him or ask if he minded the short, lumpy, uncomfortable couch. She also wondered if maybe, just maybe, he would want to share the bed, although she didn't want to push him into something he wasn't ready for.

Back at the flat she made drinks and fussed around, generally avoiding the issue until Tim yawned, a loud open-mouthed yawn that caused her to reply in kind. Unable to put it off any longer she asked the question, only it wasn't the question she had intended to ask.

"Do you want to go to bed?"

Tim stifled another yawn and looked at her with a slight tilt of his head.

"I mean, it's late and…well, you're tired. So am I. There's only one bed but you're welcome to it."

Her stilted speech along with the red blush on the parts of her face that weren't blooming into blue and yellow bruises, were clear. Tim wasn't sure how to answer straight away, his lips still tasted slightly of her strawberry chapstick from when they had kissed earlier. He had been savouring the sweetness of it, along with the feel of her body pressed against his own. She hadn't known about his past, but had been prepared to accept him for who he was – even though he knew he was not the most sociable or outgoing person in the world. Or maybe that was changing, or was going to change, he could feel something falling away as he looked at her. Someone who was comfortable being the things he wasn't and ready to help fill that gap in his life that had been empty for so long.

"We could both sleep in the bed," he answered, "if you wanted to."

Wendy didn't answer, she took him by the hand and led him into the bedroom. It was awkward, she changed into her pyjamas in the bathroom while Tim got ready and slipped into the bed. She came back into the room and saw his eyes closed and his chest moving slightly. She smiled then climbed in beside him and wrapped her arms protectively around him. In truth she was exhausted too. She fell asleep with the smell of his hair in her nose and the gentle rise and fall of his breaths pushing him imperceptibly closer to her on each intake of air.

They stayed in the flat for the next five days, during which time they did little other than make more detailed statements to Wendy's colleagues and spend time observing one another and getting to know the day-to-day habits and routines that made them themselves. By the time they were due to return to work Tim knew he did not want to go back to the house by himself; he could imagine how cold and empty it would feel to be alone again. He broached the subject with Wendy, hoping she would feel the same.

"Do you think the reporters are gone now?"

Wendy knew they had not been there since the second day when she went to his house to collect some things for him. She hadn't told Tim, partly because she was worried about him and wanted to keep an eye on him, but mostly because she liked having him there. Their relationship had been slowly growing as they spent more time together, both of them finally feeling confident and comfortable to relax and be themselves with each other. Her chest felt tight as she thought of him leaving to go back to his own home.

"I think they have now, I didn't see them last time I was there."

Tim thought for a moment then answered.

"Well, maybe I'll go back tomorrow."

Wendy was relieved that he hadn't decided to leave right there and then.

"Or maybe the day after, there's no rush is there? I don't want to be in the way."

In truth the flat was feeling more crowded than it had, which was inevitable. But it was a good crowded, sharing the space, sharing meals, sharing the bed.

"There's no rush, I like having you here."

There was another long pause as Tim braced himself to ask the question he had been mentally preparing himself for. Finally he spoke.

"When I do go back would you, that is do you think…might you want to come for a sleepover?"

He was mortified, the words that had come out of his mouth were not the ones he had intended to say, in his flustered state he had reverted to the language of an 11-year-old. He turned his face away from Wendy, finding things to look at on the far side of the room. He could hear her moving and tried not to imagine her laughing at him as she came towards him. Then he felt her sit next to him and kiss him on the cheek.

"I'd love to," she said, "I would really like that".

Chapter 33
This is the Place

Normal life gradually resumed, albeit a new normal. Tim returned home and went back to work. Wendy got a standing ovation when she returned to the police station for her next shift and they both fell into the comfortable patterns of their new relationship. As the days passed Tim started to notice more and more things about Wendy that endeared her to him, it was still too early to see things that didn't. Wendy tried staying in her own flat once or twice, only to find herself wishing she hadn't.

She didn't officially move in with Tim, she just didn't go back to her own flat much – except to collect more of her belongings, which Tim made space for by rearranging and streamlining his own possessions. Gradually Tim's house was becoming their house; one suitcase full at a time. There was no discussion about this, it just happened, in the way that plants grow without being seen or glaciers slide inexorably towards the sea.

They had been visited numerous times by Wendy's colleagues, taking statements, checking details, making sure they were okay. Crowley had visited at least three times, his concern and pride for both of them taking on a parental aspect that both Tim and Wendy agreed was touching.

One of the discussions with Crowley had been to discuss the commendations that the Chief Constable was very keen to hand out.

It had been passed to him because of his connection with Tim, to find out how to approach this without causing undue stress.

"No big ceremony, and no press," Tim told him.

"I get it, but what you did was brave and smart, you should get credit for that."
"No, it'll just be another 'brother of the missing twin' story."

"We could brief the press, ask them to not go for that angle."

"How do you think that would go?"

Crowley sighed, he knew Tim was right, he was just trying to do the right thing by everyone. Wendy came in, carrying three steaming mugs that she put on the coffee table.

"The press already ran that angle, after the arrests, it wasn't too bad."

Tim looked at her. She was right, it had not been spread over the front pages like it had when Ian disappeared. But that didn't mean that it wouldn't be. He wondered, as he so often did, what Ian would do. But he knew that Wendy had already answered that for him, he should go along with it. There was a collective silence in the room, then Tim spoke;

"Okay, a presentation. But not at the town hall or anything silly like that."

"Where then?" asked Wendy.

"I've got an idea," he replied, "give me a day or two."

Crowley raised his eyebrows and looked quizzically at Wendy who returned his gaze with a small shrug and a smile. She had no idea, but she knew that if it was what Tim wanted, she would go along with it. Crowley sipped his tea and tactfully changed the subject, becoming the first person to ask them directly if they were now a couple. He nodded his approval when Wendy replied.

"I guess we are, yes, how did you know?"

"Well, aside from the fact that you're always here – it's the matching outfits."

Tim looked, they were both in striped tops. He hadn't even noticed until Crowley pointed it out, he groaned inwardly and started to blush. Wendy and Crowley both laughed out loud; Tim joined them as the epiphany that there was actually something amusing about the constant clothing parallels hit him. He still told himself that he would make sure to check before the next time they had visitors.

After Crowley had left Tim asked if she wanted to go for a walk, to get some fresh air and exercise. Even though Wendy had already been for a run and Tim had spent half the day pushing shopping carts around, she agreed. There was something in the way he had asked her that made it more than just a suggestion.

They followed the same route Wendy had taken earlier, when she had completed two circuits of the perimeter of the park. This was more leisurely, and apparently aimless as Tim meandered towards the far corner where there were no exits and little of interest. She walked with him anyway, waiting to find out what was on his mind. She had found that it was often best to let him do things in his own time, not to push him for an answer that was sure to come eventually anyway.

They stopped in a tucked away area near the fence. The slightly too long grass here was scuffed in places, evidence of impromptu football matches having been held on the patch of green. The surrounding shrubs and bushes had evidently been cut back at some time and were growing back in spindly fits and starts, not quite enough to hide the road that ran along the outside of the green-painted fence. Tim stopped and looked around, his eyes taking in the area as he pushed his hands deeper into his pockets and pulled his shoulders forwards.

"It was here."

Wendy, having read more about Ian's disappearance now, realised what Tim meant - this was the place that Ian's bike was found, she reached her arm around Tim's waist and held him.

"The tree by the fence," he pointed to a large Beech tree, "that was where I found his bike. I used to come back here all the time, in case he would come back looking for it, or if he might still be here somehow – I don't know. I wasn't supposed to, the park was off-limits, I used to detour here when I could get away. It was always empty like this, for years, none of the other kids were allowed to play here either. By the time people started forgetting about Ian all our mates had found other things to do. I'm glad some kids come back here now, it was always a good place to meet up before….well, before."

Wendy held him tighter, knowing that there was nothing she could say that would change what had happened. She turned and looked directly into his eyes and told him, "I'm sorry, it was an awful thing. Thank you for bringing me here."

"I thought you should know, it's part of me."

"I can't imagine what you went through, but I'm glad you're sharing it with me. You don't need to keep it to yourself, just let me know if I can do anything – anything at all."

Tim leaned forward and kissed her; his face emerged with a fledgling smile and a faux thoughtful expression.

"Well, you could make me a cup of tea, that might make me feel a bit better."

Wendy stepped back and punched his arm playfully then started to walk him back towards the park gate, past the fading but well cared for flowers, benches adorned with brass memorial plaques and litter bins.

"Actually, I think it's your turn."

"But you said…"

"Well, I take it back. I demand my tea and slippers when we get home."

They stopped and kissed again before retracing their steps back to the house. Tim smiled, it was the first time in years that anyone apart from him had thought of the house as home.

Chapter 34
Prizegiving

Two mugs of tea rested on the table between Tim and Wendy, along with a small cake newly released from its cardboard home. Tim was smiling, and insisting on serving the drinks and food before he would answer any questions. Finally they each had a slice and Tim washed down a mouthful with a large swig of tea, still grinning from ear to ear.

"Come on then, what's the occasion?" Wendy asked.

"Well, you know I said I had an idea about the presentation thing, with the certificates?"

Wendy nodded and signalled impatiently for him to carry on.

"I went to see Mr Barclay today, to ask if we could do it at the supermarket."

Wendy raised her eyebrows, but still did not interrupt.

"He thought it was a great idea, he thinks it will be really good publicity for the store. I think it will be less formal than the town hall, and the whole Pick 'n' Mix Bandits thing will be a good distraction for the news, something else for them to focus on. He also said that the Chief Executive had already been asking about coming down to meet you, me and Ahmed. Apparently they want to give us a reward too, so it would get all of that over in one hit. What do you think?"

He took another bite of cake and swig of tea while Wendy ran through what he had just told her in her head. It made sense, it would be less formal and would provide a lot of secondary distractions for the press. Also, it would be in a place where Tim felt comfortable.

"I think it's a great idea too; do you want me to ask Crowley to run it by the chief? He'll be able to explain why you want it like that, and they'll listen to him. Are you sure you're alright with that?"

"I think it's the best option. Damage limitation. I know they're going to write about Ian again, even if there's no presentation at all, I'm kind of resigned to that now. At least this way there's lots of other things for them to focus on, I'll be in a crowd rather than standing out on my own."

"You know I'll be beside you all the way, you won't be standing on your own. I'll do what I can to make it easier for you."

Tim smiled uncertainly at her, he believed her but wasn't sure she really understood how hard it had been for him before. She reached across the table and took his hands in hers, a serious expression on her face.

"You know this wasn't what I was expecting, I was quite enjoying being on my own for a change. But I'm glad we found each other and I'm not letting you get away." She stopped abruptly, paused for a second then continued, "Oh my God, that sounded like a threat didn't it? I'm sorry, what I meant was – I mean to say – oh come on, help me here."

"Maybe not, I'm quite enjoying it."

"Oh you twat, what I'm trying to say is I love you."

Tim answered almost immediately.

"Good, because I love you too." This was followed by a surprised silence, they looked at each other across the table for a split second then both got up and held one another in their arms.

The presentation was agreed by all concerned. The supermarket bosses were as thrilled with the exposure and publicity as Mr Barclay had thought they would be; the chief constable was happy to accommodate Tim's wishes and the whole affair was as quiet and calm as it could be to accommodate the number of people who were interested in the occasion.

It took place in a corner of Tim's car park – with the supermarket signage clearly visible behind them – on a damp but not raining afternoon, moving afterwards to the staff area upstairs for less formal hand shaking and where Sonia, proudly sporting her shiny new engagement ring, did a sterling job of providing refreshments for everybody.

The Chief Constable introduced everybody and talked about why they were there, during which he managed to shoe horn in a subtle reminder to the press about how distressing it would be for Tim if they added too much historical background to the story, with vague reminders about how the events were not linked. Photographers and the local news channel vied for vantage points and Wendy stayed as close to Tim as she could. Many curious customers had gathered around to see what was happening, with many of them bursting into spontaneous applause once they realised what was going on and recognised Tim, Wendy and Ahmed as the focus of the event.

In spite of his nerves, and to his surprise, Tim found himself slightly enjoying being in the limelight. After so many years of trying to fade into the background and not be noticed, he found it was not as bad as he had been anticipating when he lay awake in the early hours of the morning. It helped having Wendy at his side and being surrounded by familiar faces, many of them people he had known since he was still in his teens. The spontaneous warmth and affection of their responses catching him off guard.

He felt slightly embarrassed when the chief constable described Wendy and Tim as having been injured in their pursuit of the drug dealers, a couple of black eyes and a scratched arm hardly seemed worth making a fuss over. But then, seeing how it made the reporters present bend and write frantic notes, he guessed it was another good distraction from the story he didn't want them to focus on. There was also a lot of talk about the good work Ahmed had done, which was true as none of this would have happened without him, but also helped diffuse the attention from him.

The Managing Director of the supermarket, a tall thick-set woman in her fifties wearing an outfit clearly bought especially for this event, addressed the small crowd. Although she spoke clearly and well, she was obviously nervous and stumbled several times during her short speech. Seeing this made Tim even happier that he had elected not to 'say a few words' himself when they had been planning the running order for the afternoon. She made sure to praise her three employees lavishly, talked about the supermarket's strong community ethos and thanked everybody for their diligence and hard work. She also added that Tim, Wendy and Ahmed would be receiving a generous reward in recognition of their bravery and commitment. By the time she finished everybody was ready to go upstairs and drink some tea.

Steve Barclay managed to catch Tim on his own during the general hubbub of handshaking and polite chit-chat. It wasn't too hard; Wendy had been cornered by the Chief Superintendent and Tim, far outside his comfort zone, had retreated to a safe corner. The store manager approached with a friendly smile.

"I thought that went rather well, was it okay for you?"

"It was as good as it was going to be, I hate people looking at me. Thank you for sorting it out."
"No problem, once I set the wheels in motion head office kind of took over. You're one of my best employees, even if you are woefully wasted in the car park. You just need to say if you want a warmer job, you know that don't you?"

Tim did know that, because the offer had been made many times before. He nodded, then asked, "Can my reward go to charity?"

Mr Barclay looked momentarily taken aback, then he recomposed himself and answered, "Of course, if it does we get a tax break for it, so it means we can actually contribute more – if that makes sense."

"It does; I don't need the money especially, but other people do."

"Were you thinking of any charity in particular?"

"There's one called Missing People, it helps families find relatives who have gone missing."

Mr Barclay understood, a silence hung between them momentarily before he answered.

"That would be no problem at all, I'll let the office know that's what you want."

"Thanks," Tim took his proffered hand and was shaking it when Wendy arrived at his side and took over conversational duties. They muddled their way through the next hour, standing together with Ahmed for some photos, shaking some more hands and answering questions – or rather, the same question in multiple formats. Wendy took him by the elbow and began guiding him towards the door.

"I don't think it's finished yet," he said.

"No," she replied, "but I think you've had enough, come on."

She was right, they left together, slipping away and back to the house. He was starting to get used to doing things with someone else now, although years of being mostly alone had created ingrained habits that were proving hard to break.

Walking home the long way, past the park, for instance. Or stopping to lean on the railings to wait until a train came thundering beneath his feet, shaking the stonework and drowning out all other sounds momentarily. Wendy did not comment when he unthinkingly did those things, and did not seem to expect him to explain himself to her. But he still felt self-conscious when he slipped into his old solitary habits.

The hardest to break had been transferring his announcements about the comings and goings of the day from a general despatch to the house's vacant rooms to a conversation with Wendy. On more than one occasion he had come into what he had thought was an empty house and started talking to Ian, only to realise that Wendy was at home. She did eventually ask him why he did this.

"I like to tell Ian what I've been up to, I know he's not here and I know it's silly but it's just something I've done for as long as I can remember. Sorry."

"There's no need to apologise, you can talk to Ian whenever you want to, it's your house and he's your brother."

But as time had gone on he had found himself less inclined to talk to Ian, and when he did he would just go into the spare bedroom and sit on the bed to talk in a quiet voice. It was equally hard for Wendy who had to find a place and a space in the house for herself and her belongings. Not that Tim made it difficult, it was just that she didn't want to displace anything that might be significant or important. Between them they were finding their way, as newly formed couples generally do.

Chapter 35
Surprise

On the back of the events of the previous weeks there was never any real doubt that Wendy would become a fully-fledged probationary police officer. A lot happened in a short space of time; she gave up the lease on her flat and moved the remainder of her belongings into Tim's house, making their relationship 'official'. There was a lot of reorganising of Tim's possessions and a great number of visits to the local charity shops as he shed some of the links to his past that he had been holding on to mainly through inertia. The only room that remained untouched was Ian's bedroom, Wendy never suggested it and Tim could not bring himself to consider it. The shrine of childhood toys and artefacts stayed quiet and unused.

She finished working at the supermarket when her training period began, although it had never been her dream job she felt a twinge of regret as she handed her uniform in and said goodbye to her co-workers. After all, one of the best things in her life right now had happened as a direct result of her working there. Also, she would miss her 15% discount on her shopping – relying now on Tim to grab the bargains for them.

When Tim waved her off on her training course he wasn't too worried, after all he'd lived on his own for years before he met her and she'd be back before he knew it. But he found the emptiness of the house distracting now. Putting on some music after she left, to hide the silence, then wandering from room to room, standing in the doorway briefly to confirm the absence of anyone other than himself. Then he found the first note.

It was tucked behind the kettle, written on one of the small rectangular cards that Wendy had been using for her revision notes. It didn't say much, just that she would miss him and see him soon. It was signed off with a capital W and a single x and was somehow enough to make him feel her presence. He read it several times, then went to stand it on the mantelpiece like he had done with his birthday cards as a child. But as he put it down he noticed a second card was already there, tucked half behind the clock and similarly signed W x.

As the days went by he found gradually more and more of the cards, each carrying a brief message and each signed W x. Some were in fairly obvious places, where he would easily spot them as he went about his day to day business. Others had been tucked away in more obscure spots, waiting for him to stumble across them accidentally. Some had no words, just a smiley face or a funny cartoon character and Wendy's initial. Others had useful utilitarian messages such as 'water the plants' or 'please collect my coat from the dry cleaners'. He kept them in a neat pile by the bed, with the one that had been hiding under his pillow always on top, in block capitals it said 'I LOVE YOU TIM KING.' He was still finding cards tucked inside shoes and hidden in the pages of books long after Wendy returned home from her training.

Once she was home again she had a few days spare before her first official day in uniform, she was evasive about what she had been doing with her time when Tim asked how her day had been, giving vague answers that barely accounted for the time she had spent away from the house. Tim shrugged it off, it was really none of his business how she chose to spend her time, it just didn't seem like her.

On the third day he got home from work to find her waiting for him. She was wearing a new jumper, red with black stripes, and held out another, identical one for him to put on.

"I'm not wearing it, we'll look silly."

"We always end up wearing the same anyway, let's just embrace it."

"No. I don't need a jumper on anyway, I'm indoors now."

They were both smiling and Wendy laughed as he made his token protest.

"You do, we're going for a walk."

"But I've only just got in, can't I have a cup of tea first?"

"No, because it'll be dark soon."

"I can walk in the dark, I have skills."

"Shut up, put the jumper on and come with me."

Now Tim was intrigued, it was not like Wendy to be so insistent about something. He shrugged himself into the jumper and followed her out of the door.

"Where are we going?"

"You'll see."

"Why can't you just tell me?"

"It'll spoil the surprise."

"What surprise?"

"You can't catch me like that."

Wendy led him by the hand to the park, she wasn't sure if she'd done the right thing or not, she wouldn't know for certain until they got there. It had taken a little organising and she'd had to ask for some favours from people, all she hoped was that it was okay. They walked to the corner of the park where there were some boys and girls kicking a ball around, laughing and joking as they chased it around the makeshift pitch. Tim looked around, he had seen this part of the park many times, more than he could count. He looked at Wendy and shrugged slightly.

She didn't answer, her expression had now changed from the playful excitement of earlier. She pursed her lips and pointed towards the tree, the last place anyone was sure Ian had been. His eyes followed her finger and he noticed the bench for the first time, under the tree in an ideal position for kids to pile their coats and lean their bikes while they played – which was what it was being used for right now.

He let go of Wendy's hand and walked across the grass towards it, with Wendy following several steps behind. As he approached the newly installed seat with its coat of bright blue paint a flash of light caught his eye, a reflection from the lowering sun on a shiny plaque attached to the top of the seat.

Once he was close enough to read it he stopped, engraved on the small brass rectangle were the words -

IAN KING

NOT FORGOTTEN

He stood where he was, reading the four words over and over while Wendy hung back anxiously, trying to gauge his response. Had she done the right thing? What was he going to say? Would he be upset or angry? As he turned to face her she could see the tears streaming down his face and assumed the worst, she was getting ready to apologise for what had seemed a really good idea up to this moment.

"Did you do this?"

"Yes, I used my reward money. I wanted there to be something for other people to remember him."

He turned back to look at the blue bench again.

"The council were happy to help a couple of local heroes like us. They bent over backwards."

He turned again, stepped forward and wrapped his arms around her, burying his face in the red and black stripes of her jumper while his shoulders shook. Muffled thanks emanating from the folds of wool.

"Now you've got somewhere to sit when you come here."

The end of her sentence was interrupted with a kiss, which in turn was interrupted by a football rolling muddily up to their feet. Tim kicked it back with a cheery wave as he wiped his face with the sleeve of his new jumper, then looked into her eyes.

"Thank you, nobody's ever....I mean I thought nobody....I don't know, it's...."

"Everybody cared, nobody knew what to do. As time went by they all thought it was probably best just to leave things as they were, I don't think anyone realised how much you still missed him."

It seemed inadequate now that it was there, a token gesture that was many years too late. She still wasn't convinced she had done the right thing, but as Tim walked over and ran his fingers over the inscription her doubts dropped away. He sat on the bench and patted the space beside him, where she joined him and they watched the kids playing football. They sat in silence until the sky grew dim and the two makeshift teams started to collect their belongings and run laughing to the sanctuary of their homes where their tea would undoubtedly be waiting for them when they got inside.

Chapter 36
Retirement

The following twelve months went quickly as Wendy settled into her new full-time job and they both found out more and more about one another, the good bits and the less good bits. It turned out that Wendy was not a tidy bathroom user, while Tim's underdeveloped cooking skills left a lot to be desired. Along with a great many other habits and foibles, none of which were insurmountable.

They enjoyed evenings sitting in the lounge reading as much as Tim was starting to like going out to meet people for drinks. Wendy introduced him to colleagues from her work and Tim started accepting invitations he would never have considered previously. It was different now he had someone to go with, someone who would notice when he was uncomfortable or help him out when his conversational skills deserted him. Although more and more he was finding he quite enjoyed the interactions with other people, even daring to get up and dance at Sonia's wedding.

They went together to Sergeant Crowley's retirement party, staying towards the rear of the room full of police officers who were getting rapidly inebriated. Mark joined them and as he talked shop with Wendy, Tim leaned quietly at the rear, nursing a drink and surveying the room. He was surprised when a hand landed on his shoulder, having not noticed anyone approaching. He turned to see Crowley, fresh from making his brief and well-heckled speech thanking everyone for his card and gift – a traditional wooden stand for his truncheon and an equally traditional gold watch. His expression was not the cheerful smile it had been then.

"Tim, thanks for coming tonight, it's good to see you."

"You too, congratulations."

"Thank you, you make a fine couple, congratulations to you too." He nodded his head towards Wendy, who noticed and smiled back at them.

"Tim, I know this isn't the best time or place," he gestured vaguely around the room, "but I've had a couple of drinks and if I don't say what I'm going to say now I might never have the balls for it."

Tim wasn't sure how to respond to this, was it something he wanted to hear or should he politely excuse himself? Intrigue got the better of him and he waited for Crowley to continue.

"For years I've felt like we let you down, that we should have done more to find out what happened to Ian, and I'm sorry we never did. I just wanted you to know that some of us never gave up, there were a couple of us that kept an eye open for every missing kid case or predatory individual to see if we might find a link back to Ian. It hurts me that we never got any answers for you, it wasn't for lack of trying – I hope you believe that."

Tim looked at Crowley's face, serious to the point of being severe, and then threw an arm around the shoulder of the older man.

"I believe you," he said, "and I'm sorry you never found him either. I don't think I realised for a long time how hard it was for other people too."

"You wouldn't, you were just a kid, you didn't deserve that."

"Well, I'm not a kid anymore, let me buy you a drink."

Wendy and Mark arrived at that moment and Tim ended up buying drinks for all of them, staying late into the night until the landlord tentatively suggested that everyone might think of starting to head home sometime soon, to delighted whoops of 'who you gonna call?' and much noise and merriment the throng started to head out to a swarm of waiting taxis and disappeared into the night.

Crowley had not been exaggerating when he told Tim he had never let Ian's case go. When he was clearing out his desk and sorting out his personal belongings he had pulled out a well-used notebook with yellowing tape holding the spine together, the corners were folded and page edges creased and worn. Ian King was written on the cover in blue biro which had been rewritten more than once as time caused it to fade. Inside, in Crowley's barely legible handwriting (which he had always been slightly embarrassed of) were pages and pages of notes. Every date, name and place of anything which could have conceivably been linked to Ian's disappearance in some way; a disappearance in a neighbouring county, a far off incident that bore similarities, anything concerning known local suspects. There were supplementary notes where he had followed up slender leads and possibilities, but everything had led to nothing.

There was no need for him to archive the notebook, it came under personal effects. Really it should have been sent to the shredder with other old paperwork, but he couldn't quite bring himself to let go of it. It went in a small cardboard box that came home and went straight into the loft as he got on with his new daily routines and activities.

Chapter 37
Old Friends

Crowley was back in the loft, the weak light from the single bare bulb was hardly enough to see into the corners with, he had supplemented it with a torch and was looking through, in, around and behind a selection of boxes stacked to one side of the dusty space.

As he looked he became more frustrated, swearing under his breath while he opened yet another box. He knew it was here and he knew where it was when he last saw it – at least, he thought he did. He stopped looking and stood as straight as he was able in the confined space, taking a deep breath he let his eyes scan the area.

"C'mon George," he muttered to himself, "you used to be a bloody copper, you must be able to find a box, think man."

He thought. When was the last time he came into the loft? It wasn't as if he was up and down here all the time was it? He had put a box of tapes up here a short while back, he no longer listened to them but couldn't bear to throw them out. That box was near the hatch at the top of the ladder, exactly where he had left it. He had made two trips in December and January, one to collect the Christmas decorations and another to return them. He and Jean wouldn't have bothered with more than a token effort, but their daughter had unexpectedly announced a visit with the grandchildren – leading to an explosion of glitter and snowmen all around the house.

"Bloody idiot," he admonished himself. He pulled out the boxes of tinsel and baubles enough to look behind them and there was the box of work things he had put there last year, pushed into the corner. He retrieved it and carried it downstairs where he rested it on the dining table while he made a cup of tea, then returned to rummage through and find his Ian King notebook.

He had always imagined that this box would end up as part of a bonfire in his back garden; he had not kept the bits of paper and odds and ends in it for nostalgic reasons and they served no purpose, it was just hard to imagine letting go of work completely. But the last few months had been good, with plenty of time for doing things he had always wanted to if only he had the time. Not that he was rushing around hang-gliding or playing golf, more long walks with Jean, starting an art class (which he was terrible at, but persevered tenaciously) and sitting quietly in cafés with a newspaper, watching the world pass by.

He had been sitting outside a café, the one in the park where he could enjoy the surprisingly pleasant early spring day, when it had happened. He was used to seeing people he knew when he was out, he had lived and worked in the town all his life. Some of them he could put names to, others wore familiar faces that he sometimes struggled to identify. Unfortunately, due to the nature of his work, not all of his encounters were pleasant, although his old customers usually stopped at name-calling.

On that morning a man had come and sat, uninvited, at his table. A man in his thirties with short blonde hair and a slightly crooked smile, he was well-dressed and quietly spoken.

"Can I get you another coffee?"

Crowley looked at his empty mug, then back up at the man, unable to place him.

"Do I know you?"

"You did, but it was a while ago."

There was a silence while the man continued to smile and Crowley continued to dredge his memory banks. He thought for a moment that he was going to come up blank, then it suddenly clicked.

"Collins, I pulled you for car theft, you used to run around with the Johnson brothers."

He felt satisfied at having recalled the man's identity, but was confused and slightly apprehensive about why he had come to sit with him. Frank as ever, he asked directly.

"Because I owe you a drink. So do you want a coffee? I'm getting one for myself."

Crowley's curiosity was piqued now, the man clearly wasn't planning some kind of revenge or an argument, so what did he mean? He consented to the drink, even though he knew he would regret having two in quick succession later.

"Do you remember what you said to me?" asked Collins as he put the steaming mugs on the table, "When you brought me a drink in the cell. I was really scared, I knew I was going to get time because I was still on bail from when I got caught before. Those bloody Johnsons talked me into it and I knew I was deep in the shit this time."

"I don't recall, no."

"You told me to grit my teeth and get through it, then said I should use the time to train for something so I could start over when I got out. You were kind and seemed to actually give a shit."

Crowley thought he might remember that now, he had always tried to be gentle with people in custody if he could, after all the worst had already happened for them hadn't it? – they got caught.

"And did you?" he asked.

"Fully qualified mechanic, I'm working at the garage in Fore Street. I thought it might be a good idea to use some of my 'car skills' as a starting point," he laughed as he referred to his 'car skills'. "Anyway, it was you that put that idea into my head. Once I was inside I knew I didn't want to spend the rest of my life mixing with people like that, and I didn't want to be one of those people. So I applied myself for the first time in my life. Turns out I'm not as daft as I always thought I was, certainly not as stupid as all my teachers used to tell me I was."

"Well, good for you, although it sounds like you did the hard bit yourself."

They both lifted their coffees in a mutual salute and took a long sip. The weak afternoon sun shone from behind Collins, lighting him up. He clearly wanted to tell Crowley about his road to Damascus, and he was happy to let him – success stories were rare enough in his line of work, you had to enjoy them when they came along.

"Anyway," continued Collins, "there were loads of people who would help if you wanted it inside. I got my English and Maths and learned all the basics about garage work, they even helped set me up with an apprenticeship when I was near the end. I'm planning on setting up on my own one day, be my own boss you know?"

Crowley nodded, he had often thought it would be nice to be his own manager himself. The man's first name had come back to him now, Nathan.

"Yeah, it wasn't too bad inside, not great either you know! I mean I guess it's not meant to be, but if you keep your head down and stay out of trouble it's not too grim."

Again Crowley nodded, although this time he knew Collins was showing some bravado, there was nothing nice about being inside – he had visited enough prisons to know that it was awful. He didn't say anything, just smiled and sipped his coffee again.

"No, prison was doable. Remand was fucking dreadful," he stopped and looked around, checking there was nobody sitting nearby for him to offend. "Excuse my language, but you get thrown in with every lowlife scumbag, all together in one place. I had a three-up cell with a couple of real hard cases, I was only there for nicking cars, it was horrific."

This sounded more like it to Crowley, it matched with what he knew about the system and he felt a little sorry for the young man that had been more stupid than criminal. Still at least it all worked out in the end, he finished his drink and was about to make his excuses and wish Nathan well, but he wasn't finished yet.

"I was in with a bloody rapist, he was a nasty piece of work, proud of what he was in for, I don't get that at all. The other one was no better, it was that bloke you pulled for murdering that kid years ago."

Crowley had been on the verge of getting up, he let his weight fall back into the seat.

"What kid?"

"You know, that one from years back, the one who went missing."

"Ian King?"

"That's the one, he was a nasty piece of work, I hated talking to him. I was glad when he got moved on."

"Nathan, we never arrested anyone for that."

"Oh," he appeared momentarily confused, "I thought you did."

"Why did you think that?"

"Well, one night him and the rapist got into a pissing contest about who was the worst, all bragging and one-upmanship. I hid in my bunk and kept my mouth shut about nicking a few cars. Anyway, he said that he'd done that kid in and I assumed that was what he was in for, I didn't ask – I hated talking to him."

Crowley sat across from Nathan, momentarily lost for words, then asked, "Nathan, what was his name?"

That had been earlier in the day, Crowley had hurried home and started to look for his notebook. Now he sat working his way through the pages of hieroglyphics that passed for his handwriting, looking for the name. He had recognised it as soon as he heard it, it was someone who had been on their radar at the time but they had no reason to pull him in. He finally found the page and checked, there had been an anonymous tip-off but the man had been able to produce a credible alibi when CID questioned him and he had slipped back off the radar.

Jean came puffing in with the shopping and put it on the kitchen counter.

"I thought you were going to meet me at the shop and give me a hand with this," she complained.

"Oh God, I'm sorry love I completely forgot. Sit down, I'll make you a cuppa and unpack it."

By now Jean was fully in the room, she reached across the table and turned the book so she could see the cover.

"What's happened?" she asked.

"I'll explain, but let me make you a drink first."
"I'll make the drinks," said Jean as she took off her coat, "if you've got something going on there you'd better do it. That boy's waited long enough."

"Okay, sorry – and thanks. I'll explain later, I need to make some phone calls."

Chapter 38
Good News/Bad News

Sometimes in the police force it takes an age for a lead to get followed up, sometimes they just get lost in the system or overlooked. But when the lead comes direct from a retired sergeant and is linked to a high profile case that was back in the news only recently, things happen a bit more quickly.

Nathan Collins, in his capacity as a reformed character, agreed to make a statement. Files were reopened, evidence boxes retrieved and dusted off ready to be re-examined against the new evidence that had come to light. A team of experienced officers had been hastily assembled to look into the new information around this cold case. Despite the amount of time that had elapsed, now they had a definite suspect they quickly amassed a growing amount of evidence that corroborated his confession.

Tim hung his fluorescent jacket on the hook by the door and went straight to the kitchen to put the kettle on. Wendy was on duty this evening, so he was surprised to find her sitting in the kitchen in her uniform – along with Mark and Crowley. He briefly considered a cheery hello, but their faces did not say cheery. The group wore serious expressions, all looking in his direction as he came through the door, he replaced his intended greeting with "What?"

"Sit down," Wendy said, "we need to talk to you, I'll get you a cup of tea."

Tim's mind raced, was it to do with what happened last year? Were they in trouble or in danger? Had he done something else wrong without realising?

"What is it? What's wrong?"

Wendy answered at precisely the same moment that Tim's thought processes brought him to the inevitable conclusion.

"It's about Ian."

He slumped into a chair and looked around at the familiar faces. Everyone looked concerned, they were all finding it hard to make or maintain eye contact with him.

"What about Ian? What's happened?"

Wendy put his favourite mug in front of him and he clutched it, holding it tightly as he waited for an answer. Mark spoke;

"Hi Tim, sorry to land on you like this but things have happened in the last couple of weeks, new information has come to light. I asked George – Sergeant Crowley - to come along because he was involved with Ian's case from the outset, and because he's the one who got the new information. He's helping us with this even though he's retired. George?"

Crowley cleared his throat and shifted in his seat before speaking.

"Well, more by luck than anything else, we've got a new suspect. We think it's very likely that he's the person who was responsible for Ian's disappearance."

He proceeded to give an abridged summary of his accidental meeting with Nathan Collins, and his account of his former cellmate's confession. He also summarised everything that had happened subsequently, in the short time since then. Tim sat in silence as his mind raced, a million unanswered questions, some of which may now have answers at last.

As Crowley finished up Mark took over once more.

"The thing is the CPS have said that we've got enough evidence now to charge him. Once we do that it's going to be all over the news again, there's no way we can stop that, and there's no guarantee that we'll get a prosecution or even go to court, but we wanted to let you know first, give you a heads up so you're prepared."

Tim now started to ask questions; questions about who and where and how. Most of the answers were vague, not because anyone was trying to keep information from him, but because they didn't have the answers.

No, they didn't know yet exactly what happened to Ian.

They couldn't give him a clear idea how long things would take.

The suspect was called Jeffrey Perry and was currently serving a long sentence for a series of violent crimes.

He has been questioned, but hasn't confessed. They were hoping to get more when they formally charged him and presented him with the evidence in the next day or two.

Yes, they could make a plea to the press to respect Tim's privacy – but it may not make a lot of difference.

Wendy made more tea and Mark ran through the sequence of events that would take place over the next few weeks, after which there would hopefully be more news.

"Tim, I really hope that this is it at last," said Crowley, "you've waited long enough."

"Thanks," Tim muttered, "I hope so too, thank you for keeping on trying."

He knew that was the right thing to say, and he had meant it. But there was another part of him, deep inside, that was devastated. For all the long years that nobody had known what happened he'd had hope. Hope that Ian would turn up, maybe just come strolling back into the house one day, as if nothing had happened. Or perhaps he would be spotted in a far away town, city or country, be recognised and then reunited with his brother. But dead was dead, and that was the implication of what he had just been told wasn't it? He had always known it was a faint hope, a self-delusional notion to keep himself sane. Now he felt like it was gone, all optimism extinguished.

"I just need to go for a walk, get some fresh air and clear my head," he announced. He stood up and, leaving his drink on the table, left the house hurriedly. He left the front door partially open, swinging slightly in the breeze until Wendy got up and pushed it shut.

"Will he be okay?" asked Mark.

"I don't know," replied Wendy, "but I'm pretty sure I know where he'll be. I'll give him half an hour to process things then go and find him. Is it okay if I take the evening off do you think?"

"You won't be taking time off, you'll be looking out for a vulnerable member of the public," Mark replied, "it's part of what we do. Give me a call if you need anything."

The two men left and Wendy drank her tea and tidied up; she was torn, eager to go to Tim and offer him comfort, but wanting to make sure he had enough time alone first. She kept glancing up at the kitchen clock, wishing for the hands to move faster. Finally she decided it was time to go.

Tim was sitting on the blue bench, precisely where Wendy had anticipated he would be. She walked across the grass and sat with him, taking his hand in hers. He was sitting upright, gazing into the branches of the tree, where the wind blew softly through the leaves to provide a whispering backdrop to their own stillness. His only acknowledgement of her arrival was to squeeze her hand gently when she took his. They sat like this in silence for what felt like an age to Wendy, but it was not an angry silence, there was a pensiveness to it. Not a thing you could quantify but an ephemeral, spiritual quality that enveloped them.

"Ian would have hated this," Tim whispered.

Wendy turned to look at him, to let him know she'd heard.

"Everything for him was right here, right now, he would rush, rush, rush everywhere. He could barely sleep for weeks before our birthday or Christmas, he would hunt high and low for our presents.

If our situations had been reversed he would hate having to wait to find out, even more than I can't bear it. He never did have any patience, couldn't stand counting down the days to holidays, Easter, any of it. It's why I was making a model kit and he wasn't, it's why he went off to the park before me that day, he wanted everything to be immediate so he could get straight on to the next thing."

He paused to look at Wendy, she could see his vulnerability in his eyes, in his posture, in his face, it was wrapped around him like a vine. She gripped his hand tightly, unsure what to say. Then Tim started to speak again.

"I've already waited this long, I can wait a bit longer to find out. I didn't want Ian to be dead, and while he was missing there was always a part of me that could pretend he was going to come back," he swallowed, gulping in air. "But I knew, all the time I knew really, I just didn't want to admit it. I think….I think now that….well, I'm glad. Not glad he's dead, but glad it's over although that kind of feels like the same thing."

"It's not," Wendy said simply, "you were the best brother he could have hoped for. I'm sorry, but maybe there'll be some kind of ending for you – and for Ian."

Tim let go of her hand and put his arm around her shoulder, pulling her close to him. They sat there for some time, in silence, until eventually Tim stood up and offered his hand to Wendy.

"Thank you," he said in a quiet, soft voice, "do you want to come home and I'll cook for you?"

"It's my turn though."

"You can owe me one," he smiled now and started to lead her back to the house.

He kept himself busy over the following weeks, cleaning, cooking, going to work, any activity that would help to distract him and take his mind off recent events. Realising what was happening Wendy assisted him by leaving little notes asking him to do odd jobs for her: take her uniform to be dry cleaned; deliver books to the sheltered housing in the next road; collect something she had ordered online from the shops.

The news that came arrived in dribs and drabs, and Tim didn't have to wait too long for the first to arrive. When they confronted Perry with the new evidence he confessed to the kidnap and murder of Ian King almost immediately. He was a braggart and wanted the police to know how clever and cunning he had been to evade capture for all these years. In fact, he wanted the whole world to know what a master criminal he was – and maybe in his own mind that was true.

The press were, as predicted, massively interested in the story. They dug out and rehashed all the old stories, pictures and film footage from their archives. They found out whatever they could about Perry and pestered Tim, Wendy and the investigating team for quotes and interviews.

Most of what they discovered about Perry painted an unflattering picture, an unsavoury character to put it mildly. He had been disowned by his family many years previously, had a long string of convictions and an even longer string of people – keen to be heard now - that he had wronged or hurt that had never even ended up in court. Lurid headlines and soundbite quotes sat alongside pictures of Perry and of Ian. The most popular one being the school photo that had been used at the time Ian vanished. It had been his most recent portrait and ironically could have been either Tim or Ian. The photographs that had been taken had been so similar that nobody could tell them apart. None of the usual give-away signs that their mum could use to tell them apart – Ian's dimple in his chin, Tim's scar in his right eyebrow – were visible in those particular pictures. On that day there was nothing to differentiate the two of them, even holding them up against the boys faces could not help. The fact that the picture had 'Ian' written on the back in pencil was not necessarily a reliable indicator.

Wendy helped Tim weather the storm of publicity with some success, not least due to the generous amounts of passing uniformed officers and highly visible police patrol cars in the area, which combined to reinforce the message that cold-calling and doorstepping, was not acceptable. He was offered significant sums of money by some papers to 'have a chance to tell his side of the story'. He neither needed nor wanted the money they were offering and knew from experience that whatever he said, they would write the story.

He did what he had always been doing – he waited. The only difference was that now he waited with more urgency, his patience was exhausted and all he wanted was to get to this final hurdle and see what was on the other side.

Perry was interviewed and re interviewed, but would not say what he had done with Ian's body, only that he had killed him. Like many murderers before him he wanted to make sure he got full credit for his achievements. Also, the chance of a day out to point to the burial site, albeit in handcuffs and with multiple escorts, was too good a chance to miss, a nice break from the tedium and routine of prison.

When the inevitable day came, and Perry came to show the police where Ian's remains lay, the whole operation was conducted in utmost secrecy. Wendy was tasked with making sure that Tim was nowhere near on the day. She took him to an out of town shopping area on the pretext of needing to replace some of his (their) older furniture. He had guessed that something was going on, although he didn't know what, but went along with it anyway. He had decided that whatever it was he was sure to find out sooner or later, and if it was something unpleasant he would rather put off the knowing.

Mark was tasked with driving Perry around the local area, having good knowledge of the surrounding highways and byways. Starting early in the morning Perry had been delivered to the holding cells at the station by a secure van. From there he was transferred to Mark's car, together with his accompanying burly prison officer attached firmly to his wrist. A scrawny man in grey joggers and sweatshirt with close cropped hair, a tattoo in the shape of a cross next to his left eye and a lopsided grin that showed off broken and missing teeth. They drove, with a small entourage of unmarked police cars, through the open gates and over the manicured grass, to the quiet corner of the park where Tim had found Ian's abandoned bike.

Perry made a show of sauntering around the area, towing along his guard who appeared to be ready to rein him in at the slightest excuse. Uniformed officers kept curious dog walkers at bay while the chief investigating officer asked gently prompting questions;

"Do you remember this area? Did you come in the way we did? Where did you go once you'd picked Ian up?"

Perry looked at the bench with its plaque and scoffed, causing those around him to bristle. He appeared not to notice and walked around the tree and into the bushes by the boundary where he stopped. He pointed to an area of the fence.

"There was a loose section here, I was parked on the other side. I pulled the section up and took him straight into my van."

This tallied with information that they already knew and had had suspicions about in the original investigation, the loose fence panel and the potential for getting from the park to the road unobserved. This confirmed earlier guesses that had been hypothesised.

"Where did you go then? Once he was in the van, where did you take him?"

He appeared to look pensive, nobody doubted that it was an act to string out this moment of being the centre of attention. The one with the power that came with being the only person with the information they needed.

"We drove down this way," he pointed down the street, "I took him to the old railway sidings."

Mark knew this area, it had been a run down and dilapidated place at the time Ian was abducted, the kind of place that was waiting to be reinvented as something useful after falling out of favour with Lord Beeching. Now it was a series of light industry workshops and showrooms, punctuated by small gyms and garages. He had hoped they would be avoiding more populated areas today, but it was what it was, he sighed and they went back to the car.

In the small car park outside a metal fabrication workshop they got back out of the car and repeated the same charade that had taken place in the park. Eventually Perry stopped and pointed to a rusty black pick-up truck tucked away by the side of the building.

"It's changed a bit since then, but I think that's about where I stopped. That's the place where I did it, you know? Killed him. It didn't take much to throttle the little squirt." He laughed as he finished his sentence, just a little chuckle to himself that everyone nearby heard clearly.

"Where did you go then Jeffrey?" asked the lead investigator in a gentle, almost coaxing voice. Perry appeared thoughtful, a strange look on his face as he stood staring at the pick-up. He looked as though he was living in his memories, enjoying them even. Suddenly his head snapped up, alert and ready to finish this. He'd had his fill of nostalgia and just wanted to get it over with.

"Over here," he said, walking towards the fence. He came to a halt at the chain-link and gesticulated in the general direction of the bushes on the other side. "There's an embankment, I dumped him there. I don't remember exactly where, it's just an embankment and it's probably all different now anyway. I'm done, take me back."

He appeared now to be bored with the proceedings, picking his nose with his handcuffed arm and making the prison officer repeatedly lift his own arm while he did it. Mark was happy to load him back into the car and deliver him and his minder back to the police station where he would wait to be collected and taken back to where he belonged. Mark had been appalled by his casual indifference to his crimes, the offhand way he had talked of killing Ian King and disposing of his body. Of course, Mark had come across all kinds of criminals over the years, some repentant, some confused, some even proud of their 'achievements'. Somehow meeting Jeffrey Perry had been worse than any of them, he was glad when he was finally able to return to his car and drive back to the old sidings.

By the time he got there the entire area was cordoned off, dog teams were standing by, white coated forensics investigators were arriving in droves and groups of police officers were standing around talking. Mark's arrival was what they had been waiting for; they clustered around as he gave a brief rundown of what Perry had told them and about the location of the body – which they had already figured out for themselves, but wanted to hear it anyway. Some then returned to monitoring the cordon, while others went back to their allocated tasks for the day amidst scowls, muttered oaths and shakes of their heads. Mark located the senior officer and requested permission to pass on this new information to Tim. Once it had been okayed he drove to Tim's house and waited for him and Wendy to return.

Chapter 39
The End

The moment they had arrived home, Tim carrying a large flatpack bookcase and Wendy cradling a new vase she had taken a shine to, and seen Mark waiting outside the house he had known that whatever came next was not going to be easy. The temptation to drop the new shelves and walk away was huge, a loud voice in his subconsciousness telling him that no good would come of this – just go.

He didn't, he juggled with his package as he unlocked the door and went inside as Wendy cast an enquiring glance at Mark, who nodded briefly before following them both inside. Tim started to get out mugs and put the kettle on, assuming that Mark and Wendy would want one too. He kept his back to them as he busied himself so he didn't have to see their concerned expressions as they continued to glance at one another.

Mark sat at the table as Wendy came to help with the drinks and locate some biscuits, even though she was sure they would sit untouched on the table. She saw Tim's hand shake as he poured the milk and gently put her own hand on his arm, he paused momentarily and looked at her.

"It's okay," she said, doing her best to smile, "whatever it is I'm here for you and we can do this."

This seemed to settle him slightly, he finished making the teas and together she ferried them to the table where they sat across from Mark.

"You haven't come to ask questions, have you?" he asked Mark. "What is it?"

Mark took a swig of his still too hot tea before composing himself to give a recap of the morning's events. He hoped fervently that Tim was not going to ask him about Perry; he found it hard to lie and didn't think he could bear to sit across from those haunted eyes and describe the callous indifference of his brother's murderer. If he had to, he would, but he knew it would cost him some sleep over the coming weeks, and he thought that was already going to be a scarce commodity for him.

"Jeffrey Perry has given us an indication of where Ian may have been buried. It hasn't been confirmed yet, but we're working on the assumption that it's probably true. There are specialist search teams there now."

"Where is he?"

Mark could see no point in not telling him, you couldn't keep something like this a secret. It would probably make an appearance on the local news, possibly even national if it was a slow news day.

"Do you know where the units are down by the old sidings?"

Tim knew, he nodded to Mark to carry on.

"He says he put him somewhere on the embankment at the far end, where the train tracks used to go. He wasn't very specific about where, so there's a lot of work to do to see if we can find him. If he's there they will. There are experts in this sort of thing being brought in specially to help."

The embankment, where the rope swing had been. Tim could visualise it in his mind's eye; the large tree with scuffed, bare earth under the branch with the thick knotted rope attached to it. The torn trousers and bloodied knee, and the screams of delight and terror as they took it in turns to fly over the chasm below.

"I know that place, we used to play there."

"But it's miles away," Wendy blurted.

Tim looked at her and shrugged, "We explored," he said simply.

It felt odd to Wendy now that two boys would have been taking themselves so far from home with no adult supervision. She realised of course that the perception at the time was that the world was a safer place. Right up to the point that Ian went missing and everyone started becoming nervous about letting their children out by themselves, not just here but in every town and village up and down the country.

"Can I go and see?" asked Tim.

"The whole area's cordoned off for now, you wouldn't be allowed past the police tape."

"I know, I'd like to go anyway."

"Leave it with me," answered Mark, "just let me make some calls first."

The investigating team had set up a control point close to the disused service gate for the cutting, there were strictly no press or photographers allowed in or near this area. Mark arranged with the senior investigator for Tim to be allowed into that part of the cordon, no closer. Mindful of his link to the search and the time he had waited for any information about his brother, they were keen to be seen to keep him informed.

They were met by the senior officer and Crowley, who had just arrived himself. As they explained to Tim the processes they were currently going through and what specialist teams were doing, Tim stood and stared at the trees. He watched the branches dance lazily in the cool breeze and saw the long shadows mimicking them on the muddy floor below.

Just beyond his line of sight, around a slight bend, the scrub was being diligently covered inch by careful inch, by a huge team. Spotlights had been set up in preparation for the coming night, throwing harsh yellow light into the underside of the leaves; the occasional bark of a dog could be heard in the otherwise silent wood.

"They'll keep looking all night," Crowley told him, "dig up the whole embankment if they have to. They won't stop looking."

"Good," Tim answered as he turned and walked back to the car.

Chapter 40
The Wait

Time slowed down, minutes stretched into hours and hours became endless. Tim would have welcomed the opportunity to go to work, to fill the void left in his days by the ticking of the clock. But, as predicted, the press had been covering the search thoroughly. Tim was recognisable to anyone and everyone who had access to a newspaper, TV or computer, making ordinary daily interactions embarrassing at best, impossible at worst. People would want to talk to him, wish him well, ask if there was any news or just point and whisper. He laid low in the house, relying on Wendy to bring back food and news of the outside world.

Wendy worried. She didn't want to make any assumptions about how Tim might be feeling or how he might react to this situation. She had known him long enough now to realise that he had been suffering from the trauma of the event for many years and had only recently started to function in a meaningful way – she liked to think she had helped with that, but didn't flatter herself. She hadn't 'cured' him and didn't know what she would do if he started to find things difficult again, and right now he had taken to hiding himself away. She had heard him sitting in Ian's room, his voice a low murmur under the sound of Ian's mix tapes, when he thought she was asleep. In fairness, he had done this ever since she had first met him, she had turned a blind eye as she could see how it helped him to regulate his emotions.

He was not able to concentrate for long enough to read, so today she had offered to read to him. They were currently a fair way into Jane

Eyre, she had been curled up on the sofa with him, reading aloud. Her voice had been starting to waver for the last two pages, she badly needed to get a glass of water. She looked over and saw that Tim's eyes had closed. When had he stopped listening? Had she read that whole last chapter aloud to herself? She sighed. He hadn't been sleeping well and when he did it was restless and disturbed, let him sleep now while he could. Quietly she laid the book face-down open on the arm of the sofa and went to the kitchen.

She saw a figure approaching the front door through the frosted glass and detoured to intercept the caller before they rang the bell. If it was another reporter she thought she might really let rip this time, she mentally prepared the tirade of insults that she imagined she would deliver to the hapless hack as she opened the door.

As soon as she saw Mark's face she knew what it was. She opened the door wide and let him in, simultaneously motioning for him to be quiet and to go into the kitchen. She followed him in, gently closing them in as she did so.

"He's asleep," she said in a hushed voice, "is it…?"

Mark nodded.

"Yes, boss thought he didn't need a stranger telling him."

"Fair enough, are they sure it's him?"

"Positive, they rushed the DNA from the sample Tim gave them. It's him."

Mark had no intention of going into any details about the sad pile of bones and rags that had been excavated the previous afternoon; he had been unfortunate enough to see the pictures. Perry had dug the smallest grave he could get away with, cramming the tiny corpse into the hole and covering it over. Initial examination had indicated that the body had numerous broken bones, caused when the body was stamped down into the insufficient space. The light covering was barely a few inches deep, it was a wonder it had not come uncovered years ago, but a large rock on the slope above had protected it from run-off water and an adjacent bush had grown tall and wide, stopping passing footsteps from wearing away the top layer of soil.

Wendy put the kettle on and they waited for Tim to wake. After Mark had quietly excused himself and left, she held Tim in her arms as he started to release decades worth of tears. Her own tears ran into Tim's hair as she wept for both his loss and his lost brother.

Chapter 41
Dust To Dust

There ought to have been cold rain drizzling from an iron sky as the sun prepared to come out and cast only shadows into a world where traffic was halted, people stayed indoors and no birds sang. Everything, everywhere, should have held its breath until Ian had been laid safely back into the ground. But the world carried on as normal on an early winter day which was too warm for coats, but too cold for shirtsleeves.

Ian had never had a funeral, nor any kind of ceremony to celebrate his brief life. As far as Tim could remember there had never been any discussion about this either, not while there was a chance – however slender – that he was still lost somewhere in the world. Besides, how could you bury someone when you had nothing to bury? Now that omission was being corrected. Tim stood in front of the child-sized coffin and silently said his goodbyes – taking his time and choosing his unsaid words with care.

Wendy had gently suggested the idea to him after the coroner had got in touch to ask what to do with the body. Tim was not able to answer, so she took over the phone call and asked them to hold on while they discussed it. She knew it would need to be a private affair, the media circus that would invariably accompany anything public would be unbearable. The conversation took place over several days until, gradually, the decisions that needed to be made were agreed and the wheels were set in motion.

One of the hardest parts for Tim had been who, if anyone, he could or should invite. Aside from himself there were no family members or relatives left. He did not count his step siblings from his dad's second marriage, he had only met them once and they had never known Ian. He had mostly lost contact with his and Ian's school friends, after his many years of living a mostly solitary existence, and so much time had passed that he wasn't even sure if they would remember.

The chapel they now stood in for the brief service seemed enormous for such a small number of people; the grey-haired man who quietly officiated the ceremony, Crowley – who had never given up, Mark – who came because he was their friend, and Tim and Wendy. The only other attendee was Jo Turnberry, who sat quietly and unobtrusively in the back row.

Deep down Tim had known that public interest in his and Ian's story was unlikely to abate any time soon. The news of the discovery of the body and Perry being charged with the murder had ignited another huge surge of news articles. Wendy had remembered the name of the local reporter who bought her coffee and Tim had recognised her name from those dark days. He remembered that she had written compassionately about the case, from the articles he had been unable to stop himself from reading. She had continued writing for the Echo in the intervening years, making a living and a modest name for herself. She was more than happy to be offered the chance to cover the biggest story of her life.

Between him, Wendy and Crowley they had arranged that she would have the exclusive rights to his side of the story. She had, of course, been surprised and delighted to be asked. Together they had planned access to Tim and his home, exclusive interviews and the chance to serialise her articles in the Echo, then syndicate it to a major Sunday newspaper – the articles would then be used for the book she would write about their story. All Tim asked in return was that his share of the profits would be donated to the same missing children's charity he had given his reward money to.

So far this had been working out well, with other reporters backing off and biding their time, waiting to rehash the information that she would eventually provide. Tim couldn't say he was happy about this, but knew that it was better than the alternative, the constant scrum and barrage of budding journalists hoping for their own big break. He was also finding that finally telling his story, his whole story, was having a cathartic effect. Purging things that he kept bottled up and secret for too many years.

As the funeral drew to its muted close, Wendy took a moment to hold both his hands.

"Are you okay?" she asked.

"I think I am," he answered, looking into her eyes and smiling slightly, "thank you."

"You're welcome, do you want to go home now, or are you up for a quick shopping trip?"

"Shopping trip?"

"Yes, shopping trip."

"What do we need?"

"I'm going to forgive you, because you've had a difficult day," she teased, "but you promised me that you would buy me a new dress, and you need a decent suit."

"Sonia's wedding," he answered, "I knew that. Come on then, but you get your own shoes."

He knew this was Wendy's way of taking his mind off what had been a tough morning, and he welcomed the distraction. He also acknowledged to himself that he was looking forward to the event, was in fact quite excited. He had years of socialising to catch up on, and what better way to get the ball rolling than go to the wedding of someone he had worked with for years with the woman he loved.

Chapter 42

A New Adventure

Easing himself back into a proper work routine had been a good distraction from everything that had been going on. Ahmed and Mr Barclay had been happy to see him back and his other colleagues had managed to be respectfully discreet about what had been happening. Life in the car park had returned to normal, although he had been offered a more backroom position – out of the public eye. He had politely declined, sticking to what he knew and was good at. The general public, when they were not too busy to notice who he was or recognise him, had shown restraint, compassion and kindness in their interactions with him enabling life to start to return to normal.

Home did not return to normal, it was as far from his old normal as it was possible to be. Wendy's presence was now indelibly stamped into every corner of the house, her CDs mixed with his, her pictures sharing wall space, her underwear sharing the washing line. They had grown together in a way that he would never have guessed could happen, he still had to remind himself it was real from time to time. He still had days that were difficult for him, but she was intelligent and caring and always seemed to know the best way to pull him out of it – or when to step back and leave him in it for a while, before coming to his rescue.

He had also taken on a new job, in his spare time. He had volunteered to work with the Missing People's charity, tentatively at first, as he did not feel he had much to offer. He quickly found that the empathy and understanding his situation had given him were an asset in the work he was doing. He had even discussed the possibility of training to be a counsellor one evening when He had been watching TV with Wendy. She, of course, had been enthusiastically excited about the idea as he had expected, although he had still not taken the first tentative steps towards this. He had a feeling it would not be long before Wendy returned home with a handful of college leaflets and brochures which would spur him into action.

The life that he had put on hold for so long had finally been kick-started, and although he had a lot of catching up to do, he was confident that he was now ready to finally start living - which was fortunate.

Wendy had been feeling under the weather, hungry and tired all the time, occasionally being sick, altogether out of sorts. It did not occur to either of them for some considerable time that she may have been in the early stages of pregnancy, neither of them having experienced the phenomenon at close range before. When the penny finally dropped they had a day or two of panic. Neither of them felt they had the knowledge or life experience to embark on this new and uncharted adventure. Gradually, as they both became accustomed to the idea they began to realise that, together, they would be able to do this. The more the idea grew on them, the more excited they got.

The excitement was doubled when they went for their first scan, even to Tim's untrained eye and with his lack of medical knowledge or experience the scan was clear. Twins – he could clearly see the defined outlines of two separate beings intertwined with one-another on the grainy hospital monitor.

"I guess they run in the family then," mused Tim later.

"Twins," repeated Wendy for the umpteenth time in reply. "I'll have to give up work won't I?"

Tim looked at her incredulously and gave a very slight shake of his head.

"You've only just started your job, and it's going really well. All I do is shunt trolleys around a car park, I'll look after them when you go back to work."

"Are you sure? My dad would never have done that."

"Nor mine, but we're not our parents are we? Anyway, how hard can it be?"

"Where are they going to sleep?"

"I'll clear out Ian's room, I think it's time, don't you?"

"Are you sure? I mean, I know it's important to you."

"It was important, I guess now I've got more important things to think about – you and the twins. I'll take some of the stuff to the charity shop, I may just keep one or two things though – if that's alright."

"I'd be cross if you didn't, but thank you." She kissed him on the cheek then looked into his eyes, "You're going to be a great dad you know?"

Epilogue

Steering the double buggy around the cracked pavements, narrowed by cars parked with two wheels on the kerb, was not as easy as it had always looked when he had watched other people doing it. Luckily, his years of manoeuvring trolleys through a busy car park had prepared him well for the task. He had taken to walking the twins along some of the old bike routes that he had discovered with Ian. They had changed of course, but not that much that he couldn't find his way.

Today they had cut through the park and were on their way to visit the orchard that had seemed so far away when they were kids. Now it was a fifteen minute walk, enough time to settle them after their morning rumpus. Danny had been into everything, crawling, climbing and chewing his way around the house while Freddy egged him on with his gurgled and garbled cries of encouragement. After this nap they would have enough energy to climb all over Wendy when her shift ended.

They cut down an alley at the back of some shops that would shave no time at all from the journey, but it was the way they had used to come when they cycled. As they bumped over the many potholes and skirted the rows of bins Tim noticed a handwritten sign on a piece of cardboard, he read it as he approached -

BBQs FOR SALE.

As he got closer he could see the open front of a garage and a range of stainless steel frames contorted into free standing grates that could be used to grill food if a fire was lit in the mesh basket welded underneath. They were clearly home-made, and looked as if they would be functional and efficient, not to mention elegant. They also looked familiar. Working with trolleys all his adult life, Tim would recognise the parts of them however they were dismembered and rearranged. He stopped in the doorway where an old man, who was busy at a workbench in the gloomy depths of the garage, stepped forward and cheerily greeted him.

"Out for a walk then?" he wiped his hands on an oily rag as he nodded towards the buggy before bending down to peer inside; he resurfaced with a gap-toothed smile showing through his moustache.

"Yeah, that time of day. Nice barbecues."

"Thanks, do you need one?"

"No, not at the moment, maybe I'll stop by another time though. Where do you get the parts from?"

"Oh, I take the old broken trolleys that the supermarket put out for scrapping."

Tim nodded and smiled, he looked again at the cunningly crafted objects.

"Do you know," he said, " I think I might pop by and get one some time, when I haven't got these guys with me. You have a good day."

"You too," the man smiled back as he returned to his workbench.

Authors note

Although this story and the characters in it are fictional, many people do go missing in the UK every day. Somebody is reported missing every 90 seconds – 97,000 adults and 70,000 children every year (data from the National Crime Agency report 2021-2022). The true number is probably even higher, as many cases will not be reported to the police at all.

Many of these people will return of their own accord sooner or later; they may be located by the police or by relatives. For whatever reasons, some will have removed themselves from their previous lives, others may have been the victims of unfortunate chains of events beyond their control.

A small percentage (but an alarmingly high number) will never come home. For the families and communities that these people leave behind, the effect can be traumatic and long-lasting.

When I was at school this happened to a classmate of mine, a twelve-year-old girl who vanished one sunny afternoon in the school holidays. She was never found, despite extensive searches and investigations. For everyone that knew her it remains an unresolved part of our childhood, a dissonance that we all live with. I wanted to try and articulate some of that feeling in this book, and hope I have succeeded.

If you wish to support a charity that helps those affected by this issue, or have been affected yourself, the charity 'Missing People' has a website (the information above was taken from information on their homepage) www.missingpeople.org.uk

I was born in 1964, I have three adult children a beautiful wife and one and a half cats. I live in a small coastal town in the southwest of England. I have published three novels and one novella:

Nothing Happened in 1986

Nothing Else Happened in 2011

Bloglin

Smartphone

These can all be found via my author page on Amazon.

You are welcome to write and let me know if you enjoyed this book at:

Stevebeed64@gmail.com

In return I will add you to my mailing list and let you know about any forthcoming releases.

You can follow my blog at:

https://steevbeed.wordpress.com

Printed in Great Britain
by Amazon